OVER FREEZING ALTITUDES

THE TRAVELS OF SCOUT SHANNON

KATE MACLEOD

1

SCOUT SHANNON FELT her steps slowing as she reached the end of the long white hallway that connected one airlock to the other. She was getting to the end of what had become familiar to her, and as far as she could tell, what lay beyond it was nothing. Nothing at all. Nothing but the black of space and the faint, distant twinkling of stars.

She knew the warm, close feeling she'd gotten the Tajaki trade dynasty ship had been the work of an illusion, making the walls look like wood polished until it glowed like honey, lit by what appeared to be flickering flames over brass fixtures. She didn't know what the ship looked like when it wasn't projecting that fabricated image, but even bare metal would be warmer than what lay ahead of her.

Which was nothing. Just the cold vacuum of space.

She knew that wasn't really true. If it had been true, she'd already be out in it, sucked out the end of the hallway with her fluids boiling away and cold frost creeping over her.

She had seen it happen to her friend Seeta just days before. She had felt her friend's cold-stiffened limbs with her own warm hands, and her mind could too-readily imagine what the process must feel like. Cold invading her very bones, stiffening her muscles to an icy rigidity.

But it wasn't happening, Scout reminded herself. She was walking normally through air she could breathe, and she was no colder than she normally was since she had left her warm prairies behind to travel through the corridors of space-bound ships.

Scout bent to pick up her white rat terrier Shadow, holding him tight and burying her face in the fur of his neck. He didn't need to be carried; his injury from a few days before had been slight and handily healed by the nanite the doctor had injected into his leg. But she needed the comfort of his warmth, the familiar smell of the dusty prairies of home that still lingered in his fur. Not exactly like home—it wasn't tongue-coatingly thick, capable of turning the saliva in her mouth into a gritty, metallic-tasting sludge—but enough to summon the image of days spent pedaling her bike down a narrow track in an endless expanse of red-gold grasses.

It felt like a lifetime ago. It had been barely more than a week.

Her other dog, Gert, was too large to be carried. Normally she objected to Shadow getting more attention than she was getting, but the rapidly approaching end of the hallway was making her nervous as well, and she pressed close against Scout's knee as she walked at her side, looking up from time to time with her big brown eyes. Scout bent a little to pat the top of Gert's head and try to lend her a little comfort.

Scout didn't have much of it to spare.

The six tribunal enforcers walking with her were technically human, but not the sort of humans that lent anyone any sense of comfort. It wasn't just the air of formality that radiated from their long blue robes and tall, straight postures as they walked with their folded hands hidden inside their sleeves. All of that was little different from the uniform of an officer, and Scout had known many officers who still did what was needful to put others at ease.

It wasn't their silence; Scout had grown used to that. And she had been practicing paying attention to their little gestures and glances, the rapid shifting of micro-expressions that was their chief form of communicating. Scout didn't know what they were saying, but at least she knew when they were "talking."

Yes, they were definitely odd, with their shaved heads and skin that no matter what color they had been born with was pasty, almost waxy now. They lived in deep space, far from the burning rays of sunlight

Scout had spent her whole life protecting herself against. Perhaps that was why Scout felt like they were too emotionally distant to feel any empathy for her. Their life experiences were as opposite to hers as it was possible to get.

On the other hand, people had told her the tribunal enforcers had evolved under the influence of some sort of mind-altering symbiotic organism no one had yet managed to identify. That might have been what made them seem so alien to her.

Scout's thoughts scattered away as the first of the tribunal enforcers finally reached the end of the hallway and stepped out into the beyond. The hallway connected the two airlocks; that was its function. Scout had crossed it before, from one conventional ship to another. The tribunal enforcers were simply stepping inside of their own airlock.

But to Scout's eyes, they seemed to be just stepping off into space, walking implacably forward until the dark swallowed them up.

She didn't realize she had stopped walking until she felt a soft touch at her elbow. The young tribunal enforcer, the one who had worked so hard to get her to crack the code of their unique form of communication, had deliberately brushed against her without removing their hands from their sleeves. The smile they gave Scout was not quite natural. Not spontaneous, Scout decided, a touch too formal.

But they were really trying to be friendly. Scout looked in their eyes and was sure she was right about that. They just didn't quite have the knack down. They were too used to expressions meaning so many specific things. Scout supposed trying for a friendly smile for them must be a bit like if she tried for a friendly burst of noise without making words.

So-called normal people were likely just as odd to the tribunal enforcers as the other way around, she guessed. Scout smiled back and tried to mask her anxiety.

But then she ran out of hallway and found herself standing on nothing, with nothing around her except stars scattered over a black sky, and her stomach lurched horribly.

It was worse than she feared.

And she was about to embark on a five-day journey on this ship.

She took a breath and then another step, further away from the edge of the hallway. She felt like she was falling forwards, tumbling through space, but then her foot touched the floor just as her other had, and she was standing as solidly as ever.

The young tribunal enforcer smiled that forced smile again, indicating with a sweep of their hand that she should continue further in.

Scout was about to try another step when she realized Gert hadn't come with her. She turned back to see the big black dog lingering at the end of the hallway, looking not so much frightened as confused. Scout hugged Shadow tighter in her arms, knowing that wherever Shadow went, Gert would follow.

Scout took three more steps, enough to get her to where the tribunal enforcer clearly wanted her to stand.

Gert hesitated, but only for a second. Then she bounded after, colliding with Scout's leg and falling into a sloppy sit on one hip. Her legs looked funny, sprawled across an invisible floor, her tail thumping loudly against nothing at all.

Then there was a sound, a clang, and a whoosh, and Scout looked up to see the white hallway collapsing like a telescope, appearing to shrink as it zoomed away until it was flush with the side of Bo Tajaki's ship.

Scout had never seen the outside of the ship. It was just as lovely outside as it was within, a long, delicate-looking vessel tapered on both ends like the boats that used to cross the oceans of Old Earth long, long ago. Its hull had a sheen like grayish-white marble that flashed into a burst of light as the sun rose around the planet off to Scout's right.

Her home world, Amatheon. Would she ever see it again?

Scout buried her nose once more into Shadow's soft white fur. Life on Amatheon—already not remotely easy between the frequent coronal mass ejection events forcing everyone to huddle under protective domes or deep underground and the almost futile effort to eke out crops from less-than-ideal soil—was about to get much harder if Scout failed in what she was trying to do.

And she was in so far over her head. The tribunal enforcers with their silent communions were easier for Scout to understand than the word barrages the lawyers kept launching at her.

Hopefully, the lawyers waiting to meet her at the other end of her journey on the invisible ship would be better at talking to her in a way she could understand. But even if they weren't, they were the only ones truly on the side of the people of Amatheon, the only ones who thought the people on the planet's surface and those still living in orbit around it deserved the right to self-govern. Everyone else was just focused on which member of the family in charge of the vast Tajaki trade dynasty "owned" the planetary system and was in charge of all the people who were their "employees."

Scout had never even heard of the Tajaki trade dynasty before a few days ago. She doubted more than a handful of people on the surface even knew they were supposed to be employees of the company that had funded their ancestors' journey to Amatheon more than a century before.

If Scout and her new lawyer friends failed to convince the court to leave Amatheon in peace, life was really going to change for nearly everyone Scout had ever known.

The tribunal enforcer was smiling at her again, an expectant smile Scout knew meant she was supposed to be noticing something. Scout looked around, felt a rush of vertigo as her eyes swept over distant star fields before forcing her vision to focus closer. Gert was still looking up at her, tail thumping loudly as Scout returned her gaze. Beyond Gert, she could see figures moving through space around her. Their paths described lines, and she could infer where the main corridors were, but how did the tribunal enforcers know where they were?

And yet each one she looked at was walking unerringly around their invisible ship, turning at corners and negotiating doorways without so much as putting out a hand to run along the invisible walls.

Scout looked back at the waiting tribunal enforcer. Clearly, there was some place that Scout was meant to go for the duration of the journey, and she doubted that place was lingering near the airlock. But the idea of walking in random directions until helpful tribunal enforcers or less helpful walls and bulkheads compelled her to change direction didn't seem like the best plan.

Then she remembered: she still had her AI teacher, the one she had named Warrior after the woman who had saved Scout's life during the last coronal ejection event.

"Hello, Teacher," Scout said.

"Hello, Scout," Warrior said, appearing next to the waiting tribunal enforcer. Although she looked almost exactly like the woman who had called herself Warrior, with the same long, thick, copper-colored hair and Amazonian build, she didn't look remotely like a warrior herself. Her braid was looser, her clothes softer and more comfortable, the muscles of her arms less prominent.

More like a librarian than a galactic marshal, and yet still someone you didn't want to mess with.

"Can you help me navigate this ship?" Scout asked.

"I can guide you anywhere you want to go," Warrior said. "The tribunal enforcers have allowed me access to their systems, including all ship schematics. But it would perhaps be more convenient to just adjust your glasses."

"Adjust my glasses?" Scout repeated, touching one wire bow. The glasses had been a gift from Bo Tajaki, the captain of the ship she had just left behind. They were a necessary item for her to see her tutor, another of his gifts to her. She had sort of known the glasses had other functions—the single lens she had from the real Warrior's frameless glasses had operated all the equipment on her belt—but with all the fleeing from deadly assassins and storming the bridge to hack into the communications system to get her call to the tribunal enforcers out, she had never had a chance to discover just what else her glasses did.

"With practice, you'll be able to summon up what you want by eye movements. But in the meantime, use the audio command function," Warrior told her. "Just tell it to make the walls opaque."

"Okay," Scout said, feeling intensely silly all of a sudden. She set Shadow down on the floor next to Gert, adjusted the glasses on her nose again, and loudly cleared her throat. "Glasses, make the walls opaque."

And just like that, she was encased inside a ship with actual walls, floors, and ceilings. But it wasn't metal or the illusion of warm wood tones.

No, this ship looked like it had formed out of crystal, a living crystal that grew as it chose, jutting out here, leaving a jagged gap there. Now that it was opaque, it looked like it glowed a yellowish-white from within, never so opaque that she couldn't still make out the stars beyond or the forms of people moving about within.

It was still the strangest thing she had ever seen, but Scout was immensely relieved to no longer be facing the possibility of going mad when the ship started actually moving.

She could do this. With her dogs and her AI tutor, she could get through the next five days on this alien yet beautiful vessel.

She didn't know what waited for her on the other side, but it just had to be more familiar than this.

2

SOMETHING CHANGED. Not anything she could see or hear, but something in the air, like a change in the pressure.

Scout opened her eyes, not sure if she had dreamed it or even quite what it was. But the dogs were awake too, Shadow's body stiffening as he sniffed at the air. Gert lifted her head from behind Scout's knee, tipping her big head to one side, both of her ears cocked off to the left as if she could turn them to hone in on sounds.

Scout moved Shadow away from her enough that she could sit up and reach for her glasses. She pushed back the hair that had escaped from her braid as she slept, then slipped on the frames.

"Hello, Teacher," she said.

"Good morning, Scout," Warrior said as she appeared sitting on the edge of Scout's crystallized bunk.

"Is it morning?" Scout asked.

"I'm merely calling it so because you are awake," Warrior said. "This ship has no time distinctions."

"Something just changed," Scout said. Shadow was still sniffing the air, Gert pawing to get around Scout's legs to help him find it. Scout got out from between them and dropped down to the floor. The dogs buried their faces in the tangle of blanket, but the artificial grassy smell from whatever soap the tribunal enforcers washed their clothes in was not new.

"Yes, the ship has come out of hyperspace," Warrior told her. "Most people don't notice when that happens, but you seem unusually sensitive to the effects of the engine warp field."

"Are we near the engine?" Scout asked, looking around. She could see through the crystalline walls, but it took a lot of concentration to make sense of the overlapping spaces around her.

"Not particularly," Warrior said. "And the effects were mild. You didn't ask about them, so I didn't mention. But the thing that you sensed change was the warp field collapsing when we returned to normal space. We should be in orbit around our destination in a few hours."

Scout nodded and started pulling her braid apart, finger-combing her hair before rebraiding it.

"You could tell I was feeling something even though I didn't say so?" Scout said.

"The symptoms were mild," Warrior said. "You've been more easily distracted, have shown less focus, and still show signs of not getting enough restful sleep."

"I feel like all I've been doing is trying to sleep," Scout said.

"Yes, trying," Warrior agreed.

"So less focus and not sleeping—did that affect how you scored me on those aptitude tests?" Scout asked. That had been the only thing to do besides sleep and wander the crystalline halls: let her AI tutor evaluate her educational levels and decide where to place her to further her studies.

"It was taken into account," Warrior said.

Scout would have to take her word on that. Whatever scoring system Warrior used, she wouldn't share the scores with Scout or even explain the system itself in a way that made sense. Scout knew she had missed out on a lot, having stopped going to school after her family died when she was ten. But no matter how she pressed, the AI refused to compare her to other sixteen-year-olds or other ten-year-olds or say anything that would give Scout a picture of where she stood.

"You had enough of a sense of me before to make that adjustment?"

Scout asked. She had, after all, only gotten the AI a few days before boarding the ship.

"Yes," Warrior said. "As I've told you many times, the point of my evaluating you was only to determine the path ahead, not to compare you to anyone else or any hypothetical version of you that stayed in school. My methods are not intended to measure anything, only to guide our future progress."

"I know," Scout sighed. She turned to say something more, then saw one of the tribunal enforcers standing in her doorway.

She called it a doorway, but as there were no doors anywhere inside the ship, there was probably another word that described it better. Opening, maybe? Slight narrowing where the hall turned around itself? The layout of the corridors was nothing orderly like a grid, more like the tunnels created by random paths of worms.

"Do you need me?" Scout asked. She knew they understood words perfectly well even though they never used them themselves. Still, it felt polite to make a stab at their own form of communication, and Scout put all of her polite inquiry and willingness to comply on her face. She exaggerated her facial expressions as she tried to be clear; she hoped that didn't come across as shouting.

The tribunal enforcer, seeing that they had her attention, turned and led the way down the hall. The dogs had curled back up together to go back to sleep, and Scout left them as they were. Without glasses like Scout's, they had no way of seeing the walls and quickly got lost inside the ship. After a few episodes of lost-doggy panic—one of which had ended with Gert running full tilt into a wall hard enough to stun herself despite her thick skull—they preferred to stay in the bunk unless Scout led them around on leashes.

Warrior, being an AI and therefore tied to Scout, fell into step beside her.

If the tribunal enforcers had optical implants or some other technology that allowed them to see the AI, they never let on that they knew she was there. On the other hand, they never found it odd when Scout talked to what would otherwise seem to be thin air, either.

The tribunal enforcer took her down a long, spiraling hallway to a room deeper in the heart of the crystalline structure. The floor and ceiling were far from flat, more like water frozen in gentle waves, cresting into innumerable stalagmites and stalactites.

The tribunal enforcer stopped at one such stalagmite, one that had been broken or sawed off at an angle, leaving an exposed oval that shone like glass. At first, it was like looking into a mirror that was tipped forty-five degrees away from her, giving her an outsized view of her own chin.

Then a light danced over the surface, rippling like someone throwing a handful of sand over a pond on an intensely sunny day. When it settled, she was looking at Bo Tajaki.

"Hello, Scout," he said the moment he saw her. "I hope all is well?"

Scout looked at the young man she had only known for a few days but who had become almost like a big brother to her. Despite her best efforts not to trust him or anyone else connected to the Tajaki trade dynasty, he had just seemed to understand her and see her as she was.

Right now, there was real concern in his brown eyes as he asked how she was, and she knew he wanted an honest answer.

She thought of the mysterious effects of the warp field and how she had felt odd all the way through hyperspace.

She thought of the pervasive cold that never left her bones, the tired sadness she was sure would pass if she could just feel the sun on her skin.

She thought of the thick paste that was the tribunal enforcers' only food. She assumed it was made from some sort of algae, but there was no way to know for sure. She had described the earthy, salty taste and gritty texture to Warrior over and over, but the AI's databases offered no clue what Scout was eating.

But before Scout could find a way to put any of that into words that wouldn't sound like she was complaining, Bo spoke again.

"Are you wearing a tribunal enforcer robe?" he asked. "Is that allowed? I thought it was considered a badge of office."

"I think they made an exception for me when the clothes I was wearing all turned transparent when we went into hyperspace."

Bo looked confused, but only for a moment. Then his cheeks flushed ever-so-slightly pink. "Smart cloth. You went out of range. I'm sorry, Scout. You left in such a hurry, and I never even thought to return your own clothes to you."

"I have my galactic marshal belt and a scarf from the market on *Amatheon Orbiter 1*," Scout said. "Those are still normal. I'm sure I'll get something else when we land."

She did miss the smart clothes, though. Warrior had helped her create an outfit that suited her perfectly, warm and with lots of pockets. Now she had all of her things in her belt, the pouches bulging with items that were impossible to retrieve in a hurry. Not that she was likely to need any of it on this ship where the tribunal enforcers knew what she needed even before she did, but Scout liked to be prepared.

Always being prepared for any sort of trouble had saved her life on more than one occasion.

"If money is ever an issue, please just ask," Bo said. "I can't fund the cause of these lawyer friends of yours; aside from not agreeing that their plan is the best thing for Amatheon, that would be a huge legal snarl for my own lawyers. But I can make sure you have proper clothing, food, whatever you need."

"Thanks, but I'm sure I'll be fine," Scout said. "Any news?"

"I'm afraid not," Bo said. "We are about to go into hyperspace ourselves, which is why I wanted to call. My people have searched the entire ship, but there is still no sign of Shi Jian."

"I didn't think there would be," Scout said.

"I'll have the ship searched again when we reach Galactic Central, but by my father's people. Before we dock. Just to be sure."

Scout nodded. "What about the child assassins?"

Bo flinched at the word. She didn't see him bite his tongue to keep from correcting her with the word "spies," but she sensed how badly he wanted to.

"They are still confined to quarters and are cooperating fully with my security team," Bo told her.

"They're waiting for orders from Shi Jian," Scout said.

"I don't think so. They're just kids, Scout."

"I hope you're right," Scout said.

But she was sure he wasn't. Too many of those kids had tried to kill her.

"Listen, Scout," Bo said, leaning closer and lowering his voice. "If Shi Jian somehow found a way off this ship, she could be coming after you. I'm not sure those lawyer friends of yours are going to be able to protect you."

"The message they left for me said we'll be staying at Liam McGillicuddy's house," Scout said.

"I know he's a galactic marshal and your trusted friend, but I also know he's still in tribunal custody," Bo said. "He's not getting out anytime soon. He can't protect you either."

"I'll be careful," Scout promised. "I'll keep my eyes open and my dogs close."

"And you have me," the AI tutor reminded her.

"And I have Warrior," Scout said. Bo was wearing his little round glasses that would normally allow him to see the AI, but Scout didn't know if that worked over whatever communication system was letting her talk to him over such vast distances of space.

It had taken five days to travel through hyperspace to get here; how did the communication system work? Another question for Warrior when they had a free moment. She had spent most of the last five days just trying to get a grasp on the concept of hyperspace. Warrior promised her it would make more sense once she understood the math.

Then she had shown Scout the math, full of letters and symbols, and Scout had no idea how any of that could actually be math.

"I will contact you again when I reach Galactic Central," Bo told her. "Please stay safe."

"I will," Scout promised.

She hoped she sounded surer than she felt.

"I should have sent guards with you," Bo said. "Not that the tribunal enforcers would have allowed it."

"I wouldn't have trusted them anyway," Scout said. "Not until you and your father's team sort out who is really loyal to you and not Shi Jian. Maybe not even then."

Bo's eyes darted to either side, as if making sure the room around him was clear. She couldn't see details on the crystal screen, but she could imagine the library around him. Rows of freestanding bookshelves, display cases of artifacts, dim lighting. It would be ridiculously easy to be close and yet not seen in such a place.

He leaned closer to whatever he was speaking into, probably his tablet, but Scout raised a hand before he could say a word.

"Don't say anything you don't want overheard," Scout said. "It's better to assume that someone is listening."

Bo nodded, taking a moment to reframe his words, then leaned in to speak. "I've been looking into Shi Jian. Researching her background. I told you my father hired her after she saved me from a kidnapping attempt as a child. I'm sure his people did a thorough background check on her at the time, even though, as a galactic marshal, it would be easy to assume she was an upstanding citizen with nothing to hide. My father's people are very thorough. Everything in her record looks good at a glance, but some things don't make sense when I really dig into them. Dates and locations in her background. I think the data might have been tampered with. I'll know more when I get to Galactic Central."

"If you want someone you can trust to dig further, contact Emilie Tonnelier," Scout said.

"I know she's your friend, but I couldn't convince her to choose to testify for me over my cousins in court, and my cousins are barely sane. Why would she help me now?"

"Curiosity," Scout said with frank honesty. If it seemed even remotely like someone was trying to hide something, Emilie wouldn't rest until she had uncovered everything. "Also, Shi Jian tried to kill Seeta Malini. We still don't know if Seeta will come out of her coma or ever fully recover. I doubt you'd find anyone more motivated to help you take her down."

"Noted," Bo said, and for a moment he looked pleased. But then the nervousness returned, and he glanced over his shoulders again. "Scout, whether she's spying on me or not, there is one thing Shi Jian knows for sure. Her future in the Tajaki trade dynasty is over, and there's no way she's ever going to be a galactic marshal again. She's got nothing left to lose. She's capable of doing anything. Please, please be careful."

"I will," Scout said, and Bo's image flickered and faded away.

Scout tucked her hands inside the sleeves of her borrowed robe and headed back to her room, Warrior falling into step beside her but not interrupting the confused racing of Scout's thoughts.

Bo didn't have it quite right. He thought Shi Jian had made a mistake, that Scout had used it to expose her and ruin her career.

But that wasn't what had happened. Shi Jian had exposed herself. She had wanted Scout to see her and to warn the others. Scout had nearly lost her life in the fight to get that word out.

But she hadn't. And knowing Shi Jian and what she was capable of, she should have.

Somehow, in some way Scout couldn't see, Shi Jian was still using her as a pawn. Probably Bo as well. And without knowing what the game was, Scout didn't know how she was going to thwart any of Shi Jian's moves.

But Bo was right about the last thing he'd said. Shi Jian was capable of doing anything.

3

SCOUT SAT on the floor of the space outside the airlock, a dog on a leash close on either side of her. One of the tribunal enforcers had fetched her when they had started their final approach to the planet that was her destination. To her surprise, when she reached the airlock, the rest of the ménage was waiting there for her as if to say goodbye to their guest.

Scout wasn't sure what form that farewell would take. They were still all just standing and watching her, hands tucked inside their sleeves, faces as blank as ever.

Scout was slipping her glasses up and down her nose to look at the ship around her as she had grown used to seeing it, as a thing of living crystal, and then as it appeared in its unenhanced state, which was nothingness.

The crystal ship was more comforting, but when she was floating in the nothingness, she could more easily see the planet they were approaching.

They drew closer until the white of Schneeheim filled the view below her. Details sharpened the wispy white of clouds against the grayish white of the world below as it gained definition. Some of the gray had more structure, forming long, jagged mountain ranges. The ship settled over the largest of the ranges, matching its orbit to the rotation of the world so that they seemed to be hovering in one place.

The clouds below were dense, only occasionally giving glimpses of something glinting brightly back up at them.

"The harbor ship is approaching," Warrior told her.

"Harbor ship?" Scout asked.

"This ship is not designed to enter atmosphere, not even the thin atmosphere of the port," Warrior said. "The harbor ship will bring you the rest of the way down."

"Just me?" Scout asked. That explained her feeling that the tribunal enforcers were waiting with her to say goodbye. They weren't going with her.

They weren't going to be there to explain everything that had happened to Liam's friends the Torreses. Or to Liam's family. They weren't going to be the ones to explain how he came to be arrested.

Scout's stomach tightened into an anxious fist. She knew it was all her fault. He had broken the barricade just to get to her. He'd had no reason to put his neck out like that except for a feeling of obligation to his galactic marshal partner, the woman who had died saving Scout's life.

Scout didn't know how she was going to put half of what she was feeling about all that into words, especially if they were going to be the first words she spoke to strangers. But she was going to have to.

"The harbor ship is close enough for you to see," Warrior said, and Scout was certain her AI teacher was deliberately distracting her to take her mind off her anxiety. Still, she took the distraction. She wanted to see what a harbor ship looked like before she was inside of it.

Scout leaned forward, palms pressed to the floor beneath her as she peered through the now-invisible hull. The domed city flashed now and again through breaks in the dense cloud cover. She could see the dots of ships clustering around the tops of the towers that protruded beyond the glittering dome.

She scanned the space between her and the city, looking for anything moving her way. It took her some time to find it, but once she had, she gasped out loud.

It was as white as the world behind it, but its surface was sleek against the duller cloud tops. And it was far larger than she had expected. As she tried to make sense of what she was looking at, its floating movement slowed to a halt. Then it jerked and lunged closer, the sudden movement causing the silky surface to ripple.

It was a balloon. She was looking at the top of a truly massive balloon.

A few more jerking lunges and it was even with the side of the tribunal enforcers' ship, the balloon filling Scout's view beyond the invisible airlock.

Then the gondola lifted up into view. It reminded her of Bo Tajaki's ship, its delicate lines reminiscent of boats from the past, if less decorative. Scout could see little rockets in the front and back of the ship firing, angling, and firing again, little bursts as the pilot lined up with the airlock.

"How can they even see what they're doing?" Scout asked.

"The tribunal enforcers send data to the navigational computers of docking ships. If they didn't, docking would be nearly impossible," Warrior told her.

A round port on the side of the gondola began to turn, telescoping out until it met the airlock and attached. Then both doors opened with a whoosh of air and Scout could see down the long telescoped hallway to the interior of the other ship.

A girl about her age was looking back at her, waving a greeting. Her black hair was shaved close to her head, and her arms and legs looked far too thin, as if she were fighting a wasting illness. But her face had a healthy glow and a friendly smile.

"Scout Shannon?" she asked.

"Yes," Scout said.

"Welcome to the airship Hikosen! I'm Minato. My father, Umi, and I are here to take you down to the surface. They said you needed a change of clothes. Here!"

She tossed a bundle of clothing. The bundle left her hand in a straight-line trajectory Scout recognized from her times in free fall, but when it reached the edge of the tribunal enforcers' airlock, it fell to the floor.

"No gravity over there," Scout said as she reached for the bundle and untied the sleeves of the shirt that had been holding it all together. "Wait a minute—how is there gravity here?" Scout asked. "We're not spinning."

"The two Tajaki family dynasty ships you were just on also had artificial gravity that wasn't generated by spin. Didn't you notice?" Warrior asked in a particularly teacherly voice.

"No, actually," Scout said. She could feel her cheeks heating up as she pulled on the leggings and then slipped off the robe the tribunal enforcers had lent her. Not that she was embarrassed to be naked; the AI and her dogs were the only ones looking at her, and they had seen her naked before.

No, she was embarrassed because she should have noticed about the spin. Of course, she had never seen the outside of the Months' ship, and she had only seen Bo's ship after she had left it. It made sense that she assumed they were spinning wheels or cylinders like the space stations she had been on.

"This is common, then? Artificial gravity?" Scout asked as she pulled on the tunic-length shirt and adjusted her belt over it.

"Not really," Warrior said. "The Tajaki trade dynasty is the richest in the galaxy, and the tribunal enforcers have government funding. But the technology is spreading."

"No gravity on the harbor ship, though," Scout said.

"No. And remember, the planet itself has far less gravitational pull than you are accustomed to," Warrior reminded her.

Scout folded up the robe and held it out to the tribunal enforcers. The nearest stepped forward to take it, then they all bowed together. Scout returned the gesture, feeling awkward. She could have made it look more regal if she'd still been in the robe, but the floral-patterned leggings and pastel tunic didn't have the same gravitas.

She missed her own clothes. The leggings didn't even have any pockets, and the shoes were little more than slippers.

At least she still had her belt. She buckled it around her hips, adjusting the double straps to sit one around her waist and the other lower on her hips. The pouches were all bulging, stuffed with everything she owned in the universe.

"Come on, dogs," Scout said, picking up their leashes to lead them down the airlock. They were nervous until the moment they saw the ship's interior before them, then they surged forward, anxious to return to a world that made sense around them. Scout skipped to keep up.

Then the dogs reached the end of the artificial gravity and went sailing through the air, pulling the now-weightless Scout after them while they followed diverging trajectories, making a V shape out of their leashes.

Minato caught Gert in her thin arms before she could collide with a computer panel. She slowed Gert's momentum without tumbling away herself or even losing the two-fingered grip she maintained in the doorway. Scout hadn't spent a lot of time in microgravity, but she had spent enough to appreciate this girl's mastery of moving in it.

"Sorry," Scout said as she pulled Shadow into her own arms to keep him contained. "They've been in free fall before, but I don't think they ever really got used to it."

Minato hugged Gert close to her side. Gert tried to twist around to see who was holding her. She was far more suspicious of strangers than Shadow, but she wasn't doing her low-pitched warning growl, and the hair on her back was smooth and flat, not rankled up. But she wasn't going to be satisfied until she was free, and she squirmed mightily.

She was a big girl. Minato's thin arms must be stronger than they looked.

"One of the other harbor pilots has an old shaggy dog, but he doesn't have nearly as much energy as these two," Minato said to Scout. She turned Gert around and set her moving down the long hallway that ran perpendicular to the airlock. Then she propelled herself gently across the room to lean past Scout and close the door behind her. Scout managed to half raise her hand in one last farewell to the tribunal enforcers who had rescued her before the outer door clanged shut. Then Minato closed the inner hatch, and Scout could hear the harbor ship's connecting tube telescoping shut, metallic pings and grinds echoing around her.

"Come on," Minato said from the doorway. "It's more comfortable in the cabin."

"Okay," Scout said, tucking Shadow under her arm and following Minato down the hallway, past a pair of closed doors to the main cabin at the front of the ship.

Screens showed the world around them, the crystal ship defined by the ship's computer in green lines connecting points that were defined by strings of numbers that changed as the ship receded. The planet's atmosphere dominated the screens before them, the tops of the towers under the city dome hidden in the clouds but also defined by the computer by outlines and numerical values.

Gert was hovering near something in the front of the cabin, something like a ball covered in long shanks of hair resting on top of a large, round tank that was anchored to the floor with retractable legs.

Then the ball moved to look up at Gert, and Scout realized it was a man's head. Everything from the man's earlobes down was inside of the tank. Lights were flashing in panels on the sides of the tank, and a small screen occasionally updated a list of data, adding a new line to the bottom and pushing everything else up one line every moment or two. Was it medical equipment, or something necessary to pilot the ship?

Because the tank was positioned where all the screens were converging. He had to be the one controlling things. The pilot, Minato's father, Umi. But how could he, with his hands and mouth out of view? Did he have controls unseen inside the tank?

"You're lucky; there are no storms today. Pretty calm winds," Minato said as she brushed past Scout to look at something on one of the panels. She made an adjustment and moved on to the next panel. "It's a short trip. We just have to sink down to match altitude and then glide in."

"I've never been on a balloon before," Scout said. She didn't feel like they were sinking, probably because she was still floating weightless in the air. Minato went to her father's side and murmured something to him as she caught hold of Gert, then towed the big black dog back to Scout.

"They are pretty unique to Schneeheim as harbor ships," Minato said, pushing Gert over to Scout. She hooked a foot around a handle set in the floor so she could remain near Scout and the dogs. Scout had an arm around each dog, which left no hands to spare to hold herself steady. Minato caught her elbow to gently hold her in place.

Scout felt like she was being assessed and guessed that while Umi piloted the craft, Minato made sure the passengers were comfortable. She gave Scout a reassuring smile and continued speaking. "Schneeheim was very volcanic in its past. At the same time, it's so small its gravity is only about a third of standard. That makes for huge mountains. The tallest peak is nearly higher than the atmosphere here at the port city. Perfect for high-altitude airships. Airships combine balloons, where the atmosphere is thick enough to float, with small rockets for where it's not."

"This is only the second planet I've been to," Scout admitted.

"Me too," Minato said with a sudden smile. "I was born on Agate, nearer to Galactic Central. I haven't been back there since I was eight, though. I can't handle full gravity for long, and my father not at all. But don't worry, I can manage just fine on Schneeheim. I'll be taking you through processing and handing you off to the Torreses, who are waiting for you."

"You know the Torreses?" Scout asked. Relief started to bubble up inside her. She could ask Minato all about them, get a sense of who they were before she met them. But then Minato shook her head, and that momentary feeling of relief evaporated in a flash.

"Not personally," Minato said. "They arranged for my father and me to pick you up. The tribunal enforcers don't really talk, you know."

"Yes, I know," Scout said. She must have sounded more miserable than she felt because Minato's hand on her elbow gave her a little squeeze.

"Long journey?" she guessed. "It's nearly done, and I'll be with you the rest of the way. You're not alone here."

Scout mustered up a smile and hugged her dogs. Clearly, that silent journey had been too long, leaving her too much time to worry. The Torreses were Liam's friends and had put themselves at risk just as he had done, all to get Scout off her world before festering hostilities erupted into outright war. They had to be good people.

Scout just wasn't used to depending on others. It felt unnatural to have to do it now. But she knew she wasn't alone.

Of course, she had the dogs. The three of them would get through all this together, even if two of them didn't actually know what was going on. It was a comfort just having them there with her.

No one with dogs was ever alone.

4

SCOUT, a dog tucked under each arm, propelled herself out of the cabin doorway and back down the hall to the airlock. She made a long arc down its length, touching down halfway to her destination. The next bound only took her half as far, and from there she was taking something closer to steps than sailing jumps.

Gravity was coming back faster than she had expected. She set the dogs down and let them walk the last bit of the way.

There were no screens in the airlock room, no way to see what was happening as the floor bucked under her feet and she caught hold of the doorway to keep from falling to the ground. They buoyed back up, then dropped again, shimmying a bit from side to side.

Scout closed her eyes and willed the rising bile taste at the back of her throat to subside. She really didn't want to throw up. Who knew where that would all end up if she did.

The floor dropped away beneath her, startlingly fast this time, and Scout yelped out loud.

"It's all right," Minato said, finally following Scout to the back of the craft. Scout opened her eyes to see Minato smiling at her as she made her way down the hallway. Metallic braces on her legs rang loudly with each step, and she was leaning forward over a pair of canes in her hands. Her face was flushed, and she was winded even by that short walk, but her smile never wavered.

"You said there wasn't a storm," Scout said.

"Oh, this? This is gentle skies," Minato assured her. "Although you do look a bit green. Don't worry, we'll be docking in just a moment, and then you'll be standing on firm ground. You'll feel better in a jiffy."

Scout nodded, hoping it was true but not trusting herself to speak as another shimmy of the ship around her brought the bitter bile taste back.

Minato seemed to know the instant the directional rocket was about to fire, putting out a hand to catch Scout before she could lurch back and gently supporting her until all of a sudden, they were perfectly still.

"See? Better already," Minato said, braces clanging as she crossed the room to open the airlock doors one after the other. "We'll be outside, but only for a moment. Just keep following me, and you'll be fine." Scout nodded, adjusting the dogs' leashes in her hand, then followed Minato out of the airship.

Although they were once more moving through the telescoping attachment to the airlock, it wasn't sealed on the other side, just locked down to the edge of an open platform. Scout was momentarily blinded by all the whiteness, a bright sun dancing through wisps of white cloud that skittered over the platform and swirled all around them.

Then there was a break in the clouds, and she saw just how high up they were, over the top of the glistening dome. Under the dome, Scout could see clusters of towers, all of enormous height, all with their tops a long way beneath the platform where she stood.

Scout felt a momentary wave of vertigo, a sensation like she was already tumbling forward, although in fact she wasn't even standing close to the edge at all. Then a sudden memory hit her, of being on another platform high above a cityscape on *Amatheon Orbiter 1* and Geeta—with the intentions of saving her from certain captivity—throwing her over the side. She had landed a few meters later in a safety net, but for one eternal moment, she had thought she was going to fall for the rest of her short life.

"Scout, I need you to keep walking," Minato said to her, a commanding tone in her voice that compelled Scout to open her eyes and take a step closer to that voice. "The air is thin out here, and you haven't adapted to it yet. We need to get you indoors. Just keep walking, you'll be fine. I've got you."

Scout took another step and felt Minato wrapping an arm around her, her walking stick dangling from her wrist as she hugged Scout close. She had to put her weight on Scout, but there wasn't much of that, spindly as she was, especially not on this planet. She guided Scout across the platform to a large set of glass doors.

Then they were inside, out of the wind and clouds. The doors closed behind them, and Scout took a deep breath so full of oxygen it made her dizzy. But that feeling quickly faded, and she felt her mind sharpening.

"Better?" Minato asked, and Scout managed a nod. Minato let her go and fussed a moment to get her cane back in her hand. Scout looked down at her dogs, who were both breathing in tongue-lolling pants. If the thinness of the air had bothered them at all, they were at least recovering quickly.

As Minato led the way, Scout realized they had not yet reached the top of the tower itself, only an enclosed part of the long ramp where they had docked. The view of the city was still dizzying, but being out of the wind with the clouds forced to pass around the glass enclosure and not blow around her all wet and cold was a definite improvement.

The bounteous oxygen helped, too.

The hallway ended in a large room that felt almost star-shaped, with all the other ramps bristling off from its central core. The ceiling was a single glass dome, and Scout realized as she looked up at it that so far she had only been looking down at the long drop to the city below.

The view up was even more dizzying. There was no sky, only the faintest wisps of clouds stretching and dissipating in long, thin tendrils and, beyond them, the starry expanse of space. Occasionally something out there winked at her, a distant ship drifting in orbit.

"We really are above the atmosphere here?" Scout said.

Minato looked up as if she had forgotten there was something up there. "Most of it," she said. The central core of the room was a bank of elevators that sensed their presence and opened their doors invitingly.

"Does the gravity get stronger as we go down?" Scout asked as she led the dogs into the elevator.

"No, why would it do that?" Minato asked, pushing the button to close the doors and then leaning against the wall to rest. Her face was flushed, and she appeared nearly out of breath.

"That happens in space stations with spin, I guess," Scout said. "Although the one I was on, the change was so slight I didn't notice it. But they said some people did."

"Huh. Never heard of that," Minato said. "Interesting."

"Are you all right?" Scout asked. "Do you need help, or to get back to your ship? I could probably find my way from here—"

"No, I'm okay," Minato said, pushing away from the wall as the elevator slowed to a halt. "I know I look like I'm beat from just that little walk, but that's good for me. I actually have a set number of hours I'm supposed to spend on the surface every week, and I'm a bit low at the moment, so taking you around works out perfectly for me."

"Someone schedules your time?" Scout asked.

"My doctor. It's important to move about in gravity as much as I can for as long as I can. Someday I'll probably end up like my dad, floating in a pressure tank and never able to come back out. I'm trying to push that day as far into the future as possible. Sorry, I know it's a bit much to watch for some people."

"Don't apologize," Scout said, feeling her cheeks flush furiously. "I should apologize to you if I made you feel self-conscious at all. You shouldn't have to explain yourself to me."

"It's all right," Minato said. "I'm used to it."

Scout racked her brains for something more supportive to say. "I don't really know what it's like for you, but I can see you're working hard to make the best of it. I totally respect that. I knew someone back home who had a hover chair. She got around with it just fine, but she was looking for work in free fall where she could move pretty much like everyone else."

"That's kind of why my father and I are here," Minato said. The doors opened, and she led the way down another long hallway. Scout could hear voices from behind some of the closed doors, and more voices in some larger, more echoey space ahead.

Minato stopped at one of the doors and knocked softly before opening it and stepping aside to let Scout and the dogs go in first. The dogs lunged forward, always anxious to explore a new space, but Scout felt a prickle up her spine, every hair on the back of her neck suddenly standing on edge.

She kept a firm grip on the leashes as she looked up and down the hall. Back the way they had come, it was still empty, every door closed, all the way back to the bank of elevators. In the other direction, she could see someone dressed like a doctor walking quickly away from her, eyes on a tablet in his hands. A pair of men not dressed like medical staff were talking together, arms crossed and laughing, not looking her way.

They didn't look familiar to her. But something had. Someone had. For just a moment, she could have sworn someone was watching her. Someone with blue-gray eyes in a shade she could never forget.

Eyes just like Clementine, the laconic girl assassin who had tried to kill Scout back on Amatheon. Who would have succeeded, too, if not for the heroics of Scout's dog Gert.

But it couldn't be Clementine. Aside from them being a five-day journey through hyperspace away from Amatheon, Clementine was dead.

"Everything all right?" Minato asked.

"Yes," Scout said. She could hardly say she'd just seen a ghost, especially as there was no sign of anything now.

But still, the prickly feeling of being watched didn't leave her.

She followed the dogs inside the room and let Minato shut the door behind her. It closed with a satisfyingly heavy click. It might not hold up to an actual attack, but it was enough to separate her from watching eyes.

Yet the feeling of unease lingered. It couldn't possibly be Clementine back from the dead to haunt her, but the fact was that Clementine had been an assassin trained by Shi Jian. Was Scout's subconscious trying to give her a warning?

She would have to mention it to the Torreses when she met up with them, even if it only made them look at her like she was crazy. She needed someone else to know.

This snowy little world just didn't feel safe.

5

SCOUT VAGUELY REMEMBERED doctor visits when she was a child, but after her parents died and she was left on her own at age ten, those had become a thing of the past.

Until a week ago. Now she had been inside so many examining rooms, medical pods, and other doctor-related spaces she was heartily sick of them.

"Hello, Minato," said the woman who was already in the room. She looked like a plump grandmother with rosy cheeks and long white hair in a braid wrapped several times around the crown of her head. She smiled at Scout, then at each of the dogs in turn. "Scout Shannon and company. I'm Dr. Schneider, but as we're all friends here, you can just call me Heidi. I'm all ready for you; this should just take a moment."

"This is about the thin air?" Scout said as Heidi turned to look at some items ranged out on her counter and compare them to something on the computer tablet in her hands.

"Mostly," Heidi said, turning back to Scout with an injection gun in her hand. "It's a bit of a nanite cocktail, but nothing like what they give you on really inhospitable worlds. Part of it is to nudge up your blood's ability to function in low oxygen. There are also some monitoring nanites to be sure your organs don't start showing stress from either the low oxygen or, more likely, the low gravity. But you're young and healthy; I really wouldn't worry about it."

Scout held out her arm and Heidi pushed the sleeve a bit higher on Scout's biceps before pulling the trigger. Scout felt the pressure, but it was far less painful than the loud crack of the gun made her expect.

"What happens if the monitors detect a problem?" Scout asked. "I have smart glasses, but no implant."

"The nanites will send an alert to me, and I'll come find you," Heidi said, setting down the injection gun and picking up a smaller version of the same. Shadow, who knew what Heidi was after the moment she bent down towards the dogs, scuttled to hide behind Scout. Gert, as usual caught unaware, became dog patient number one with an indignant yelp.

"I'll reload, you catch the little one," Heidi said. Scout bent to pick up Shadow, whose attempts at fleeing were only getting both of them hopelessly tangled in his long, fine leash. In the end, he found himself trembling in Scout's arms as Heidi injected the nanites into his rear flank.

"How long before we feel the effects?" Scout asked.

"This building and most of the transport systems have increased oxygen pumped in, so you won't have a chance to notice it until you get outside of those systems," Heidi said. "In most cases, patients don't feel any different at all. I've given you a bit more than usual since I'm told you'll be leaving the city at some point."

"I guess I might. The McGillicuddys live in a village part of the time. So, is that it, then?" Scout asked, rolling the sleeve of the floral-printed tunic back down.

"Nearly," Heidi said, looking over her tablet again. "Your medical records were forwarded by Bo Tajaki, so we know there's nothing to be worried about there."

Scout didn't know what to say to that. She had no idea she even had medical records. But she had been put inside a pod after Shi Jian had nearly choked her to death. Scout supposed, in addition to healing her injury, it had given her a thorough examination. That, or he had accessed the earlier one that had been done on her back on *Amatheon Orbiter 1*. Or both.

"He even forwarded clothing preferences. Very thoughtful of him," Heidi said.

"Clothing preferences?"

"You'll need weighted clothing to help mitigate bone and muscle loss while on this planet," Heidi said. "We have printers that fabricate them to generic specs, but in your case, they are making them to order even as we speak. The dogs will have weighted vests. Most dogs find those comforting. Wearing the vest feels like a hug."

Scout's head was spinning. She suspected Bo Tajaki had sent some money to Schneeheim as well. She doubted she was getting all of this care and attention for free.

"And Minato, how are you doing?" Heidi asked.

"Same old, same old," Minato said with a smile. "It's actually feeling a bit better since you tweaked the braces. There's less rubbing."

"That's good to hear. We'll take another look when you're in next week. You might not believe it, but you are having a growth spurt. You'll never be as big as your brothers, of course, but you'll still be a damn sight taller than most survivors of Hachet's disease."

"I don't know why I'd want to be any taller," Minato said. "It makes my bones ache."

"Just when they're growing. Give it a bit of time. It's good to see you keeping up with the exercise."

"Yes," Minato said, fussing with her walking sticks, and Scout sensed she would rather discuss it without Scout and the dogs as an audience. "Well, if you're done here, I'll take Scout to the printing station?"

"That's fine. It was nice to meet you, Scout and... dogs. I hope you enjoy your time at Schneeheim."

"Thanks," Scout said, not sure that "enjoy" would be the correct word.

Minato led the way back to the hallway and further down, closer to the sounds of voices. There were other people in the hall, a few dressed like medical workers and most looking a little lost, clearly going through processing much like Scout was.

Minato said something, but Scout couldn't focus on the words. She had the sudden intense feeling of being watched again. She spun around, but no one was there. Just a pair of people walking the other way, lost in a whispered conversation. Scout stayed where she was, eyes sweeping over every doorway, every cross hall that might be a place for a spy to duck off into.

It felt different from last time. She had no sense of those blue-gray eyes on her. Was she being watched by someone else this time?

"What is it?" Minato asked.

"Nothing," Scout at last admitted. "I felt like someone was following us."

Minato looked down the now-empty hallway. "Well, that wouldn't be weird. Everyone's processing ends at the printing station, and it's just right here."

Scout glanced the direction that Minato was pointing but turned back to make one last search of the space behind her.

The dogs looked up at her quizzically. Clearly, nothing was setting off their alarm modes. Scout must be overreacting.

But she didn't think she was.

Scout followed Minato into a long room. A counter ran along the left side of the room, and behind the counter was a wall filled with cubbies, some empty and some containing little piles of folded clothing. The backs of the cubbies opened up into another room beyond, and Scout could see people working on the other side, setting the clothing into the empty cubbies while massive machines whirred away behind them.

"Here," Minato said, stepping up to the counter and catching the attention of one of the employees with a wave of her hand. A girl of about their age came over, a polite smile on her face.

"Scout Shannon," Minato said, pointing back over her shoulder at Scout. "And dogs."

"Oh, yes!" the girl said, looking down at a data display on the counter before turning to find the appropriate cubbies. She came back with two vests for the dogs, one slightly larger than the other, and a veritable mountain of clothing for Scout.

"So much?" Scout said. She could no longer see the girl behind the counter, not through the pile of weighted clothing.

"We had orders," the girl said. "There's a bag in here somewhere as well. If you want to take it all over to one of the changing rooms, you can get it all sorted."

Scout looked around and saw that the right side of the room was all doorways leading into closets with mirrors, a chair, and a counter on the far wall.

"Thanks," Scout said, somehow getting the entire mountain into her hands and staggering into one of the changing rooms. Minato followed after, awkwardly carrying the dogs' vests by looping the armholes over her wrists.

The weight must have been agony for her. Scout quickly dumped her load on the counter and ran back to help.

"I'll wait out here," Minato said. "I'm just going to poke my head out into the waiting room and see if your friends are here."

"Thanks," Scout said and shut the door.

She got the dogs dressed first. Gert was delighted: her vest was a deep blue color and covered with overlapping images of daises. Her tail wagged at a blurring speed as Scout adjusted the straps around her.

Shadow was less pleased, letting Scout know in a series of subtle muscle twitches that weren't quite jerking his paws out of her hands that he wasn't pleased with this putting-on-clothes business. His vest was a uniform black and had a matte quality that would likely make him truly invisible when standing in shadows. Normally, his white fur glowed ghostly in all but total darkness.

Scout found the bag first and sorted out what she was going to put on and what was going in the bag.

"Hello, Teacher," she said, summoning her AI as she pulled on a pair of pants that were nearly identical to the ones she had created for herself out of smart clothing back on Bo's ship, but heavier and warmer because of the weighted cloth.

"Hello, Scout," Warrior said, appearing out of nowhere to lean against the counter. "How are you finding Schneeheim?"

"Did you know about this clothing thing?" Scout asked.

"We determined your preferences back on Bo's ship," Warrior said. "I was interfaced with the ship's system at the time. Do you find it a breach of privacy?"

"No," Scout said, realizing she hadn't really thought about it that way. Perhaps that merited more consideration later. "No, what I meant was, we only designed one outfit. There are like twelve here."

"The components are designed to mix and match," Warrior told her. "I would estimate you have more than a hundred unique options for completed outfits with what you have here."

"But how?"

"Extrapolation from your stated preferences," Warrior said. "Of course, the longer you interact with me, the better I'll know you. You do like these clothes, correct?"

Scout pulled a vest with dozens of pockets on over her ribbed turtleneck sweater, then added another warmer shirt over the top. The colors were all browns, blacks, and beiges.

"It's perfect," Scout said. "I just wish I had a hat."

"But there is one, just there," Warrior said. Scout moved a stack of sweaters into the bag and found a knit cap of bulky gray yarn with flaps to cover her ears.

Not exactly what she was longing for, but she had lost her father's bush hat. Even if she created a new one just like it, it wouldn't be the same.

Scout pulled on the knit cap, then stuffed the last of the clothes in the overfull bag. She slipped her stockinged feet into sturdy boots lined with warm, soft fur-like fabric and tightened the straps.

Then there was nothing else to do but meet the Torreses. She opened the door and peeked out to find Minato waiting for her.

"All set?" Minato asked.

"Yes, thanks," Scout said. "I've never gone anywhere feeling this prepared for everything that might happen. I even have goggles in this bag."

"You'll appreciate those if you get caught out in a storm," Minato said. "Nothing worse than blinding snow freezing to your eyelashes. Or so I've heard. I stick to the tower tops myself."

Scout slung the bag over her shoulder and grasped both of the dogs' leashes. The girl behind the counter gave them one last wave and then they were out of the printing station and in the large echoey space filled with benches and throngs of people all waiting for ships to arrive or depart or for friends or family.

Minato guided Scout to a corner of the space where two people were waiting near one of the immense windows looking out over the city. They weren't enjoying the view, though; their heads were together as they spoke earnestly in hissing whispers, then fell silent as they saw Minato and Scout approaching.

"Hello," Scout said, moving the leashes to her left hand so she could extend her right one. "I'm Scout Shannon."

"No time for pleasantries," John Carlo Torres said, ignoring her outstretched hand in favor of relieving her of her bag.

"We have to run," Mary Grace Torres told her. "You are in too much danger here."

Before Scout could say anything at all, not even goodbye to Minato, they each took hold of one of her arms and propelled her through the waiting room crowd, the dogs yapping excitedly as they were dragged along behind.

Scout twisted her head around to catch one last glimpse of Minato leaning on her sticks, the white expanse of cloudy sky over the tower tops of the city behind her.

Then the Torreses pulled her down another corridor, and Scout was lost among strangers.

6

THE CORRIDOR ENDED in what Scout recognized as a train platform. She had taken many trains on *Amatheon Orbiter 1*, but those had all been under the surface of the city, in the bowels of the space station. They were still on the same level as the processing station under the docks, further down than the top of the dome, but still higher than the tops of the other towers. How could there be a train up here?

And yet a row of cars stood waiting, people scurrying on or off as a buzzing announcement and chiming bell said they were nearly out of time. Mary Grace scooped Shadow up in her arms and ran for the last of the train cars. John Carlo still had a grip on Scout's arm and forced her into a run to follow. Gert galloped along beside her, head swiveling as she took in the activity around her.

Gert was definitely getting more used to crowds than she used to be. Instead of being on edge, she seemed only a bit disappointed no one was noticing how pretty her vest was.

The doors slammed shut behind them, and Scout staggered as the car jerked forward before finding a smoother acceleration.

The car was smaller than the ones she had traveled on before, only large enough for the three of them plus the two dogs. There was a bench against the back wall where Mary Grace had collapsed with

Shadow in her arms. Behind the bench was a curved window, and Scout could see the train platform disappearing behind them.

Then she was blinded by intense white light, blinking as she realized they had emerged from the tower and were following a narrow track that curved away from the building.

"Where are we going?" Scout asked.

"We have to get you down the mountain straight away," John Carlo told her. "We had intended to keep you here with us in the city at first, but that's not possible now."

"What happened?" Scout asked.

"People are here," Mary Grace told her. "People who have been asking about you. That's not good. No one should even know you are here."

"What people?" Scout asked.

"We're still working on that," John Carlo said. "We should have some answers soon, or possibly just better questions. But in the meantime, we're taking you to Emma McGillicuddy."

Scout felt suddenly dizzy in a way that had nothing to do with the motion of the vehicle under her. She reached out to touch the wall of the car, then followed it down until she was sitting on the bench beside Mary Grace. Gert flopped down on top of Scout's feet and Shadow stretched out from Mary Grace's arms to lick at Scout's elbow.

The Torreses must have sensed she needed a minute. Mary Grace put a hand on Scout's knee, and John Carlo turned toward the front of the car to have a whispered conversation through some sort of communicator.

Scout hadn't consciously made a mental picture of the two, but she realized that part of her had formed an expectation of who she would be meeting. They were lawyers, after all, and she had seen entire squads of lawyers every time Bo had met with his cousins, the Months.

The Torreses were nothing like those lawyers. They weren't wearing flashy, tailored clothing with neat haircuts and the latest wearable tech.

No, the Torreses looked like farmers. And Scout realized that was probably just what they had been, back before the Tajaki trade dynasty had taken over their world. They had become lawyers out of necessity, but they hadn't bothered conforming to all the trappings.

Scout looked down at the hand on her knee. That was a hand that was still making time to dig in the dirt, to brush up against hot engines or get splashed with jelly cooking at a rolling boil. Scout had never been a farmer herself—her parents had been bakers—but she had lived among them most of her life.

To her immense relief, she felt comfortable with the Torreses.

Then the car started to slow, pulling up to the next station, and she felt both of them tense.

She might be comfortable with the Torreses, but she was still in danger.

"I felt like someone was watching me back at the processing station," Scout said.

John Carlo turned to give her a sharp look through the untidy length of his salt-and-pepper hair. "That is a highly regulated area," he said. But he didn't sound like he doubted her.

"I think it might be one of the assassins trained by Shi Jian," Scout said.

John Carlo's eyes widened in surprise. He glanced at Mary Grace, who shrugged, her eyes just as puzzled as his. Scout opened her mouth to further explain when they were once more plunged into darkness.

"Head down," John Carlo said, even as Mary Grace was putting a hand on Scout's back to guide her into putting her head between her knees. Shadow whined a complaint at being pushed aside. Gert looked up at Scout's face looming over her, then up at John Carlo, who had moved to stand at the door, prepared to block the way with his body.

Scout stayed quiet as the doors hissed open and the sound of a busy platform beyond filled the train car. She heard laughter, voices calling farewell, someone playing a wind instrument in a swooping, dancy melody.

A moment later, the doors hissed back shut, cutting out the sound, and they continued on their journey.

"Two more stops," John Carlo said. "Then we change to the tram."

"What's the tram?" Scout asked.

"Like a train car but suspended from wires," Mary Grace explained, and Scout remembered that like her, John Carlo and Mary Grace had grown up on a much lower-technology world than anything in Galactic Central. They didn't make her feel foolish for asking basic questions.

"The McGillicuddys are in a hamlet at the end of the tramway," John Carlo told her. "A winter home for a collection of herders. Not a big town, but with winter coming on, it's not as desolate as in summer."

"And I'm going to hide there?" Scout asked.

"No one would think to look there," John Carlo said. "Or so we thought. The city should have been safe enough for you, but bad people are out looking for you."

"We have contacts in the criminal element here," Mary Grace explained. "Someone is paying for any information on your whereabouts. As far as we can tell, you aren't meant to be harmed, but normally there would be a specific instruction to not hurt you, and the orders as they've been relayed to us have no such instruction."

"We could be getting a garbled version. Or an incomplete one. We're not sure. But to be on the safe side, we're sending you down the mountain," John Carlo said.

"What if they follow me there?" Scout asked.

"It's too small of a town," Mary Grace said. "There is no way they could hide there. Even one person who doesn't belong there would be noticed. You'll see when you get there."

Scout nodded, then hunched over in the seat again as they drew into another station. When the doors had once more shut and they had plunged back out into the white light, she slid sideways in her seat to look out the back window.

The rail the train ran on was so narrow it was hard to make out its path further back than the building they were just emerging from, but then Scout's eyes caught a glimmer of light reflecting on metal and followed it around.

The train ran in a slow spiral, plunging through each tower at a slightly lower level than the last. She wished she could see up ahead. Would they stop at ground level?

John Carlo turned away to have another whispered conversation, and Mary Grace opened a bag she wore close to her side to offer Scout a sandwich. Scout took it with a nod of thanks, aware of both of the dogs' eyes on her as she took a bite. Soft bread spread generously with a dark-colored nut paste, slathered with such a thick layer of honey it was spilling around the sides of the sandwich. Scout had to twist her hand repeatedly to lick at the backs of her fingers and catch the sticky trails before they reached the cuff of her coat.

She didn't mind. The honey was like sweet golden sunshine, so exactly what she needed after days of the tribunal enforcers' strange food. And the places where the honey had soaked into the bread crust while still wrapped in Mary Grace's bag had crystallized like candy.

Scout was sticky when she was done, but the dogs were eager to help her clean up the last few sticky spots on her hands. And when the dogs were done, Mary Grace handed her a napkin to wipe off the dog spit.

"Nearly there," John Carlo said, moving to stand by the door. Scout hunched over, listening to the sounds of people on the other side of John Carlo. She wished she had been able to walk through the city; everyone in the stations sounded so merry, like it was a holiday and they were all celebrating together.

Then they were back in the silence of their car and then back out into the sky.

Only it wasn't so bright here, and Scout saw that they had spiraled so low she could see the streets below, the cars and bikes and people. There was a marketplace full of light and color as hundreds of shop signs all competed for her attention.

The streetlights were decorated with banners, each a silver snowflake on a bright blue background. Some of the bags the shoppers carried had similar patterns. Maybe it really was a holiday here.

"This last station connects to the tramway as well," John Carlo said. "Just stick close with Mary Grace, and we'll move through as quickly as we can. We're catching the last tram of the night. Once we're on board, everything will be fine."

For the night, anyway. But Scout didn't say that out loud.

The doors opened on an even greater roar of sound, lots of people moving about through an even larger space, echoes filling the vaulted ceiling above them. John Carlo went first, finding breaks in the crowd for Scout and the dogs to follow. Mary Grace stayed close behind Scout, head constantly swiveling as she looked all around them for any signs of trouble.

Scout wanted to look too, but it was all she could do to keep the dogs calm and close at her sides through the crowd. She kept them both close to her left side, Shadow between her and Gert, as he was the one more likely to be trampled on. She had a vague sense of the room around her: large, the only windows high above offering nothing more than a glimpse of white sky, the walls all cold gray stone.

Those walls felt old, like someone had found the remains of an ancient city and put a layer of modern city over the top of it. But she didn't think that could be true. With the low gravity and low oxygen levels of the atmosphere, no one could have lived here before they had the technology to enclose everything under a dome, could they?

John Carlo reached back to catch hold of her elbow to guide her through one last thick throng of people to a separate room off the main hall. The ceiling still vaulted high above her, the windows offering only cold, remote light, and the old stone still surrounded her, but there were considerably fewer people here.

And in the middle of the room was an immense machine that held a system of cables aloft. The cables disappeared through a hole in the stone floor at a steep angle. Even as Scout was trying to peer down into the large rectangular opening in the floor, something rose up through it, dangling from the wires and rocking softly as it came to a rest at the top of the wires.

The machine stopped turning, and the voices around her settled to a quieter level, no longer shouting to be heard over the racket of the machine.

"This way," John Carlo said, leading her to the doors in the side of the tramcar. The doors opened but only four people trickled out. One appeared to recognize John Carlo and greeted him with a smile and a nod. John Carlo nodded back, his smile more of a thin-lipped grimace.

Then they were on the tramcar. Scout brought the dogs to the back corner and got them both to sit beside her.

Mary Grace paused in the doorway, one hand resting lightly on the door frame as she looked over the crowd, occasionally rising up on tiptoe. Scout suspected a pantomime; she wanted to look like a woman looking for a lost companion and not someone trying to suss out a shadow.

But if it were really Shi Jian and her girl assassins gunning for Scout, the subterfuge wouldn't matter.

Scout felt that prickling being-watched feeling again and looked around, scanning as quickly as she could, desperate for a real glimpse of whoever was watching her. Had she really seen blue-gray eyes, or had she only imagined it?

But she could see no one looking their way, and when the doors closed, they were the only ones in the tramcar.

"Is this weird, being alone?" Scout asked.

"Not at all," John Carlo said, and indeed, he looked far more relaxed now than at any moment since she'd met him.

"So everyone pretty much lives in the city?" Scout asked.

"Oh no," Mary Grace said, still with that gentle tone of voice that said that none of Scout's assumptions were silly in any way. "There are many villages, but most are on the southern slope of the mountain. It's less rocky there, more suitable for the winter sports and other visitor highlights. The village we're going to is on the north side, colder and darker and too steep and rocky for anything but goat herding."

"They make fantastic cheese," John Carlo told her, his dry tone at odds with his word choice. Scout was getting the sense that John Carlo was a very serious sort of man. Probably a good thing in a lawyer fighting a seemingly unwinnable battle.

"I know you're from a warm world, and this isolation might be hard for you," Mary Grace said. "We'll bring you back to us just as soon as we safely can. Hopefully, before Schneeheim. That's the winter festival here. It lasts for three days of feasting and dancing and games. The city is actually quite nice. It has all the modern amenities of Galactic Central but feels more like the sort of world we're used to. I'm sure you'll have the time to explore all of it while we build our case."

"I don't mind being alone," Scout assured her. "But seeing the city does sound nice."

Scout looked out of the window. The world around her was already dark, the sun still shining down on the city blocked here by the mountain itself. Everything below was all jagged rock and silvery snow and long, impenetrable shadows.

She hoped she would be back in the city soon. But if there was one thing that seldom worked out for her, it was hoping for a thing.

She was just going to have to get used to this new, dark world.

7

SCOUT RESTED her head against the window and watched the mountain slope pass below her. The glass of the window was pleasantly cool, and the rocking of the tramcar was like a cradle trying to lull her to sleep.

Then she saw light below and snapped out of her doze. The sun had completely gone, the ground below her had lost all definition, but directly in front of the tramcar, where the cables were descending to, was a cluster of bright lights.

"The hamlet," John Carlo said. "Most of the homes are close to the station, and there is a market there on good-weather days. The lights are around that. The McGillicuddys actually live a little further up the slope, but they are meeting us at the station with lights, so you won't be walking alone in the dark."

"Alone?" Scout asked. "Aren't you staying?"

"We can't," Mary Grace said, putting a hand on Scout's shoulder. "We have too much to do, and the communication systems down here are spotty at best."

"But you said this was the last tram of the day," Scout said.

"Yes. We'll say goodbye from here. But there will be enough time to introduce you to Emma and the kids," Mary Grace said.

Scout nodded, then turned back to watch the lights drawing ever closer.

As they reached the end of the line, Scout saw John Carlo and Mary Grace both adjusting their clothing, tugging on knit caps and turning up their collars. Scout dug her own cap out of her jacket pocket and put it on, smoothing the ear flaps down over her ears.

The tram car lurched to a halt and swung for a moment before the doors slid open. For a moment, nothing seemed different. Then a gust of wind danced inside the car, carrying flakes of snow with it, and Scout gasped out loud.

She had slept out at night in the prairies of Amatheon on many occasions. More than once, she'd woken to find a fine layer of frost clinging to her blanket. Those had been cold nights.

Or so she had thought at the time. As Scout struggled to zip her own collar up over the bottom half of her face, she realized her idea of what cold was had been off by several orders of magnitude.

"Scout," John Carlo said, holding out a hand for her to step up beside him. Scout clutched the dogs' leashes and led them to the edge of the doorway.

The tram platform on this end wasn't in an enclosed room. She could see a flat surface beneath a fine dusting of snow, although if it was stone or concrete, she couldn't tell in the yellow-toned light.

The platform was one side of a large open square, probably where they set up the market. The other three sides were all houses, squat structures that also appeared to be made mainly of stone, with low doors and no windows.

Waiting on the platform was a woman and three children, too bundled up in warm clothing for her to make out any details.

"Scout Shannon, this is Emma McGillicuddy and her children Willem, Trevor, and Neil," John Carlo told her. "They're going to take good care of you."

Scout bit her lip, not sure what to say. To her dismay, the garbled loudspeaker voice was already announcing the tram's departure, and the chime was sounding.

"We have to get back," John Carlo said, "but we'll be in touch. And the moment we're sure it's safe, we'll send for you."

"Thank you," Scout said.

Mary Grace pulled her into a tight hug that ended with a gentle push to encourage her to step off the tram. She did, the dogs jumping down after her.

Then the doors hissed shut, and the tram rose back up the mountainside. The Torreses inside were still waving back to her when the tram reached a point too distant for Scout to make out any more details.

She turned to face the family that was missing a member thanks to her. She held the dogs close to her side. Shadow was fine with this, shivering and picking up his paws one after another, not liking the cold radiating from the platform. Gert, on the other hand, was straining at her leash, desperate to run and explore, pushing her nose through little drifts of snow with happy snuffles.

Emma McGillicuddy pulled down the scarf that had been wrapped around her face. Her cheeks went from pink to red at the first touch of the cold air, and Scout thought she had a clue why no one seemed to want to be the first to speak. "We should get up to the cabin. It's warmer there, and we can talk."

"Okay," Scout agreed, then tucked her chin deeper into her collar. She found gloves in the pockets of her coat and moved the leashes from hand to hand as she pulled them over her fingers, which were already turning a ghoulish sort of white in the cold.

Then she followed the row of figures that stepped off the platform into a trench dug in the snow. The snow on either side was nearly a meter deep, and Scout was glad they didn't have to walk through that. Plus, the walls of the trenches protected them from the worst of the wind.

Then they reached the last house at the edge of the little hamlet and the end of the neatly dug trench.

Emma helped her children clamber up onto the snow. Scout tried to climb up after, but Shadow made a little whine, and she went back to pick him up. Gert was more willing to plow through on her own, eager even. Scout let go of her leash, trusting she'd stay nearby. Gert plunged into the snow like a dolphin in water, throwing great masses of it up into the air to slowly drift back down in the low gravity, or more often, to be carried away on the wind.

The wind was cold, but it was nowhere near as strong as the wind Scout was used to back home. She guessed that was because of the thinner atmosphere.

Plowing through the snow was hard work, but she was only a little winded, so the nanites must be doing their job keeping her blood oxygenated.

The hamlet had been built on a plateau, but Emma led them to the edge of that plateau and then up the slope of the mountain. The wind was more prevalent here, if not exactly strong, and had swept the rock nearly clean of snow, making the walk easier.

Scout realized they were following a path of sorts when they passed through a deep fissure in the rock where someone had fashioned stairs to help at the steeper bits. Beyond the fissure was another open slope, this one so steep that Scout had to put her head down and focus on taking step after step as the muscles of her legs started to burn.

She hoped she wouldn't have to make this walk again, except to get back down, and surely that would be easier. Even pedaling her bike over the hills back home hadn't been this much work.

Then the slope ended on another plateau with deep piles of snow. Scout lifted her head and saw a light shining from over the door of a little stone cabin on the far side of the plateau, Emma and her line of children spread between her and it. Gert came galloping past Scout to plunge once more into the deeper snow. Shadow watched her go by, then shivered as if he felt the cold Gert didn't seem to notice at all.

The others were waiting at the front of the cabin for Scout when she arrived, the littlest child stomping their feet, perhaps from the cold or perhaps from impatience. Emma opened the door and led the way into a small room not unlike an airlock, closing the door once they were all inside.

Then the family began shedding outer clothing, and Scout finally saw them all. Each of the boys had red hair like Liam, although where his had been thinning and cut close to his head, theirs was thick and wavy like their mother's dark blonde hair. Scout guessed they were all between ten and six.

Scout unzipped her jacket but left it on. Even with the shirt, vest, and second shirt, the air still felt cold. So far, the indoors didn't feel all that much warmer than outside.

"We have food," Emma said as she opened the far door and warm light from the home beyond filled the coat room. "Soup and fresh-baked bread. And lots of hot tea. The best thing for warming back up." She tried to smile at Scout but was frequently distracted by her three children barreling past her into the kitchen. When the last of them had gone, she bent to pick up the hats, scarves, and gloves that had fallen helter-skelter to the floor and put them in the cubbies over the coat hooks.

"I'm sorry," Scout said.

"Oh, it's all right, dear," Emma said. "I don't mind the cold, and it's good for the boys to get out now and again."

Scout had to puzzle over this for a moment before she realized Emma thought she was apologizing for making them meet her at the station. "I meant for Liam."

"Oh," Emma said, and her cheeks colored. "Oh, there's nothing to apologize for there. We talked about it before he left and we both agreed that he had to go get you. We owe Gertrude Bauer so much, both of us. And we knew he would almost certainly be arrested and might be unable to continue working as a marshal even if he was cleared. We made the choice together, and I don't regret it, not a bit. I know he doesn't either."

"But now you have to hide out here, so far from home," Scout said.

"It's not so bad," Emma said and tried to muster up a convincing smile. The smile faltered, and Scout was afraid she was about to break down into tears, but to her surprise, Emma burst into laughter. "Okay, I hate it here. There, I said it. So cold, so dark, so remote. But it's the safest place for the boys, who think it's just grand they get a bonus break from school. And it's not forever, is it?"

"I hope not," Scout said.

"Come inside," Emma said. "Let's get some warmth inside of us."

The food was just as warming as Emma had promised, and tasty besides. The soup contained potatoes and corn, two things Scout knew well, but it was mainly cream, something she had never had before. The bread was light and crusty, and there was a huge crock of butter to smear over it, the golden pats melting the moment they touched the steaming bread.

Once the food was all gone, the boys scampered away, Emma calling instructions after them. "Neil, pick up your toys before bed. Willem, double-check your homework before you transmit it to your teacher. Trevor, I'll be along in a moment to help you with math, but at least take a stab at it without me."

All three groaned loudly in protest, but Emma just poured herself and Scout another mug of tea.

"Your dogs are very well-behaved," she said. Scout looked down at Gert, flopped down as usual right on top of her feet. Shadow was sitting at attention nearby, clearly hoping for a few table scraps and not deterred at all by no one paying any attention to him.

"They're good dogs," Scout said. "They're my family."

"Have you thought about your future once you're done testifying in court?" Emma asked.

"Not really," Scout said. "Bo Tajaki gave me an AI teacher, and I've been working on getting my education level up to where it should be. Or trying to work on it. Things have been chaotic a lot. But I know with an education I'll have more options."

"Yes, you will," Emma said. "Of course, I'm biased. I'm a teacher as well."

"Really?"

"Yes. I teach science to kids between nine and thirteen. It's a very exciting age."

Scout nodded and tried for a smile that wasn't too halfhearted. In her experience, that was a good age for molding kids into killers. But surely that wasn't the only thing a kid could learn how to become.

Not that she knew herself. She had spent those years working for every meal and missing more than a few when work was scarce.

"When you're done with your tea, I'll take you out and show you where you'll be sleeping," Emma said.

Scout took a deep gulp of tea, lemony and sweet, then asked, "Out? I thought I was staying with you."

"You can if you like—I can convert that couch to a sleeper—but I thought you'd like a bit more privacy. And quiet, something that's in short supply here."

Scout didn't doubt that. Whatever tasks the boys had been assigned must still be waiting for them; it certainly sounded like some sort of throwing and tackling activity was going on its place at the moment.

Scout swallowed the last of her tea, then gathered up her dogs and zipped up her jacket while Emma put back on the layers of her own clothing.

Then they were back out in the cold night, although it didn't seem so bad this time with a belly full of warm food and tea. They trudged through the snow around to the back of the cabin, then a little further uphill to a second, smaller cabin that stood on a rocky promontory, the door on the side facing the hamlet below. Emma punched a code into the lock and then opened the door, stepping aside to let Scout and the dogs in first.

It was definitely smaller than the other cabin, all one room with a little screen dividing the shower and toilet from the rest of the space. A bed piled high with thick blankets and an overstuffed chair sat on either side of a dark metallic box that looked like some sort of stove, and opposite the bathroom was a tiny kitchen with a single cupboard over a sink and just enough counter space for a little kettle.

"This was Gertrude's," Emma said, her voice going soft. "She was Liam's partner, but she was my good friend."

"I'm so sorry for your loss," Scout said.

"Thank you," Emma said. "I can see why she liked you. At any rate, when her grandmother fell into a bad way, Gertrude gave everything she had in the world to take care of her until the day she died. Gertrude was left with nothing. Working as a marshal, she was always traveling, but when she was off duty, this was her place. Liam and I had to make her take it. Proud doesn't begin to describe her. But I know she loved it. I think you being here is just what she would have wanted."

"I hope so," Scout said.

"You'll see in the morning, when the sun comes up, why she loved it so. Whenever you're up and ready, just come down the hill, and I'll fix you something to eat. There's tea and coffee in that cupboard. I'll have to scrounge up something for the dogs to eat besides the scraps the boys were giving them under the table when they didn't think I saw."

"They what?" Scout asked. She hadn't seen any of that. Emma laughed.

"Don't worry, nothing dangerous for dogs or I would have said something," she said. "I better get back before they destroy something. If you should go out, the code to get back in is just five-five-five-five. I can show you how to change that tomorrow. Good night, Scout."

"Good night, Emma. And thank you so much."

Emma smiled again before wrapping the scarf once more around her face and pulling the little door to the cloakroom closed behind her.

Then Scout heard the deeper boom of the outer door closing, and she and the dogs were alone.

8

SCOUT AND THE dogs curled up together in the little bed under an enormous pile of blankets. The dogs conked out at once, exhausted from their big day, but Scout lay awake for a long time listening to the sound of the wind whispering around the cabin walls. She hadn't realized how much she had missed the sound of the wind. She wasn't sure she ever really paid attention to it back on Amatheon.

The wind on Schneeheim never built up to the sort of gusts she was used to, just the soft sound of driving snow plinking against the walls. It was a cold sound, but she was warm and cozy in her thermal underwear with the dogs near her.

Scout woke with a start, both dogs fighting to get out from under the covers. She didn't know what had set them off. They both ran to the door, barking like mad. Shadow stayed at the door barking his shrill bark over and over, but Gert came back to the bed and put her paws up on Scout's knee as if requesting human assistance with the door.

Scout stumbled out of bed and turned the lights on. She didn't know what they were so excited about. It was impossible to hear anything over Shadow's noise.

"Shadow, hush!" Scout said. Shadow paused, but only for a

moment. Scout heard nothing unusual in that little break before he started barking and scratching desperately at the door again.

Perhaps he simply needed to go out. Scout put both the dogs on their leashes, then led them through the inner and outer doors.

Somewhere south of the mountain, the sun was rising. She could see the gray light lighting the world around her, although the actual sunrise was blocked by the mountain itself. The dogs pulled on their leashes, barking over and over, and Scout took a step forward before remembering that she needed to be wearing a lot more clothing to be comfortable outside.

She started to take a step back, and in that moment's distraction, the dogs got away from her. The leashes whipped out of her hands, and both dogs charged across the snow. Scout saw a flicker of motion: some small, gray, furry animal running for cover. It disappeared inside a rocky prominence jutting out of the snow. Shadow desperately tried to dig after it, ignoring the chill of the snow on his paws in his desperation to get at the animal. Gert stood behind him, not looking at anything in particular.

Scout knew this procedure well. Shadow would be tenacious, never giving up until he had what he was hunting for. Gert would seem not to care much one way or another, or even to really understand what was going on, but half the time she was the one that ended up with the small animal in her jaws. Scout was never quite sure how that happened.

The wind from the night before had died down, and the dogs didn't seem uncomfortable, so Scout went back into the house to put on the rest of her clothes before joining them outside. She didn't bother sorting through her bag, just put on what she'd been wearing the day before and then all her outer gear. She wasn't sure how long the dogs would be safe alone, and she didn't want to dawdle.

When she got back outside, the gray had become brighter, but the sun was still out of sight. The mountain seemed to have a glow, and Scout suspected that the sun would emerge soon and maybe warm up the air a little. The two dogs were just as she had left them, Shadow whining to himself as he spun round and round the promontory of rocks trying to find a way in, Gert looking around in a way that didn't really suggest that she was protecting them from possible ambush so much as reacquainting herself with the world, getting distracted by the occasional snowflake.

Scout walked over to the two dogs, and Gert rushed up to greet her, landing on her hard with both of her front paws. Scout staggered but didn't fall. Gert, tail wagging madly, moved to jump on her again, but Scout dodged away. Gert charged back to Shadow's side.

Maybe it wouldn't be so bad, stuck out here on the lonely mountainside. She really needed to put the time in to train Gert better, or at least to teach her not to jump up on people, and now she'd have it. And she needed to get going with her AI education as well. She might as well start both today.

"Scout!" Emma called.

Scout walked to the edge of the cliff to look down at Emma, waving to her from the door of her own cabin. Scout waved back, then whistled until both dogs came running to her. Shadow skipped sprightly over the frozen top layer of snow. Even with the weighted vest on, he was light enough not to break through the thin layer of ice.

Gert, on the other hand, had no such luck. She tried again and again to hop up top where Shadow was making such good time, but she kept crashing through the hard layer and had to just plow her way back to Shadow and Scout. It might have been a lot more work, but judging from the wagging of her tail and all the snow clinging to her nose, she loved every bit of it.

Scout caught hold of their leashes and led them down to where Emma was waiting for her.

Emma was standing out in the cold with her coat open and no scarf covering her face. That was the first clue that something was wrong. That and the deep furrow between her eyebrows.

"What is it?" Scout asked. Emma's cheeks were bright red from the cold, but she didn't seem to notice. She must be very worried.

"We have a call," Emma said.

"The Torreses?" Scott asked.

"No, Bo Tajaki," Emma said.

"Bo?" Scott asked. "How could it be Bo? He's supposed to be in hyperspace now."

"I think that's why he's calling you," Emma said, letting Scout and the dogs through the door first before shutting it behind them.

Scout dropped the leashes and opened the inner door, and the dogs rushed inside to the excited squeals of three boys in the middle of breakfast. Scout loosened her scarf and unzipped her jacket, then went into the cabin and looked around for whatever served as communication equipment. Willem saw her looking around and pointed even before his mother emerged from behind Scout to lead the way.

There was a little desk in the wall, set into a little nook. Scout slid into the seat and saw that the surface of the desk was a screen set at a comfortable viewing angle. A look of immense relief eased the tight anxiety of his features, but only for a moment. He looked like he hadn't slept for days.

"What is it?" Scout asked.

"The kids are gone," Bo told her.

"The assassins?" Scout asked. Emma nudged Scout's shoulder, and Scout moved the chair closer to the desk so that Emma could pull a screen across the opening of the nook. Scout understood; her kids didn't need to hear this.

Bo had flinched at the word again but said, "Yes, the assassins. And worse, I don't know when they escaped. They spoofed the video feeds. We found the bodies of the guards that were supposed to be watching them stuffed in a utility closet. We were nearly two days into our five-day journey, but there is no sign of anyone hiding on this ship, and none of the shuttles are missing. The logs for the airlocks say no entry or exit since you left, but of course, those must have been tampered with. I'm afraid they left before we ever even went into hyperspace. I'm really afraid they left with Shi Jian, and none of us noticed because we could still see them on the security monitors behaving perfectly normally. But Scout, I think they're coming after you."

Scout nodded. She wasn't shocked or surprised. In a way, it was really a relief. She'd been waiting for this hammer to fall for quite some time. "Don't beat yourself up too much. They can be like ghosts. That was how they picked us off before. They're invisible to security measures. You never see them until it's too late."

"I believe you," Bo said. "Can you get somewhere safe?"

"I guess I'm as safe here as I can be anywhere," Scout said.

"I'm changing course," Bo said. "I'm coming to get you."

"No, don't do that," Scott said. "I have everything I need here. I have people who will look out for me. There's nothing you can do for me here. You need to get Galactic Central, to get your father's people on the case, and not keep getting sidetracked."

"This is all my fault," Bo said.

"You met Shi Jian when you were quite young, right?" Scout asked. Bo nodded. "She got inside your head. She knows how to do that. She knows how to work kids at that age. It's what she does. I think it's pretty much all she does. Aside from killing people, of course."

"I will do as you ask," Bo said. "But tell me again, are you sure you will be safe?"

Scout nodded, she hoped with more surety than she felt.

"We'll be going back into hyperspace then. Three more days. So I'll call you again in three days. If I can't reach you, I will be coming for you. If it means that I have to take a little ship and come just on my own, I'll be coming for you."

"Understood," Scout said. "Be careful too. I don't think Shi Jian would do you any harm, but I'm not sure if she's working alone. She might have a partner, and who knows what that person might do. They might not value you the way she does."

"I'll know more when I get to Galactic Central," Bo said. "I've sent as much information as I could through secure channels to my father. I haven't heard back from him yet, but that's not unusual. When he is working on a thing, he doesn't communicate about the thing. But, as I promised, I'll talk to you when I get back home."

"Safe travels," Scout said.

"You too," Bo said.

The image flickered to a dull gray, and Scout sat back in the desk chair. Then she opened the screen to find Emma waiting just outside.

"The assassins are kids between ten and fourteen," Scout told her. It wasn't hard to keep her voice lower than the chatter coming from the breakfast table. "More than two dozen of them. If they do come here, they will be noticed, right?"

"Yes," Emma said. "We're close with the people in town, and they know the broad strokes of your situation. If any of them see anything, they'll send a warning right away. We can lock down this cabin like a fortress. You do realize, Liam is a fifth-generation galactic marshal. Sometimes trouble follows a marshal home. His family takes all the precautions, always have."

"Good to know," Scout said.

"Are you hungry?" Emma asked, guiding her back to the kitchen. "I have something for the dogs now, and there's porridge. If you want it."

"And brown sugar and raisins and pecans and dried cranberries too," Trevor said.

"That all sounds really good," Scout said. She sat down at the table, laughing along with the boys as the dogs jumped all over Emma before she could even lower the two bowls to the floor. The dogs tucked in with great gusto.

Scout dug into her food, not much more slowly. She hadn't realized how hungry she was. She was just finishing a second bowl when a beeping sound from the desk behind her had her turning in her chair. It sounded like a warning.

Emma held up a finger to let her know to stay where she was, then crossed the room to sit down at the desk. She leaned close and whispered with the screen. Scout looked down at the remains of the porridge in her bowl, no longer terribly hungry. But she might need the energy later if things got bad. She spooned more into her mouth.

A moment later, Emma came back to the table. She poured herself a large mug of tea with extra milk and sugar, then another for Scout.

"It's bad?" Scout asked.

"It's not… what's concerning you," Emma said. "It's the weather."

"Storm?" Trevor asked. He sounded entirely too excited about it.

"A bad one," Emma said. "They're evacuating the town."

"Evacuating the whole town?" Scott asked.

"There's a possibility that the storm will take out the tramway," Emma said. "That's happened before. It's procedure to evacuate the population of possibly affected villages beforehand, just in case. It's probably nothing, and we have a little place inside the city for just such contingencies. We'll just have to find a way to hide you. Keep you all bundled up in your coat and hat and scarf and you'll blend in with my children. If we're lucky, no one will notice you. Once we're safely inside the apartment in the city, we can just keep you hidden indoors there until this blows over or the Torreses can come get you."

Scout didn't know what to say. It felt like such a coincidence. And yet there was no way that Shi Jian and her assassins could be controlling the weather. It had to be a coincidence.

But it felt more like a trap, driving her back into the city. The warm city, snug under its protective dome, but full of dangers just for her. Shi Jian and her assassins might not have created the storm situation, but they were surely prepared to use it to their advantage.

And there was nothing Scout could do about that.

9

IT WAS MIDMORNING when they were finally ready to head down to the village. Scout didn't bother to hold the dogs' leashes. They both came when she whistled, and there were no other people around to object to dogs on the loose.

The sun emerged from behind the mountain, shining dazzlingly bright off the snow. Scout dug through her pockets until she found the pair of tinted goggles she had put there the day before. She hadn't known what their purpose was except possibly for fashion when she'd put them in that pocket, but it was obvious now. Looking around for more than a minute or two at that snow would be blinding.

This time, there were people in the public square. Not many, maybe not even so much as fifty, but they were all heading to the tramway station. Scout looked up the mountain towards the city and saw the tram swinging on its line as it made its way down the slope to them. It seemed to be empty, but she couldn't shake the feeling that the inside was teeming with young assassins bristling with knives and murderous intent.

She looked around the town. The people were clustered in family groups, some of the clusters chatting with each other. She saw mothers adjusting the clothing of their children, fathers wrangling toddlers closer to the platform. Just normal people.

The tram reached the platform, and the doors opened. There was no one inside.

The people at the front of the line started boarding the tram car, filling up the back corners first so there would be room for the others. It would be a tight fit, but they would all make it.

Emma and her family were near the back of the crowd, waiting patiently for their turn to board. Scout stood a little farther away, watching the dogs sniffing along the snowy trench that led to the edge of town.

Then Scout felt it again, the prickling sensation that she was being watched. She turned and looked everywhere, carefully examining every corner of every cabin, every trench dug through the snow, every rocky prominence that jutted from the ground. Anywhere that could be cover for someone lurking, Scout watched intently but saw no signs of motion.

But she was sure. She was sure in her gut that trouble had already come for her.

"Come on, Scout," Trevor called to her. He and his family were already on board the tram. Only Scout lingered on the platform, Scout and her dogs.

"It's okay, Scout," Emma said. "We're among friends here. We won't use your name once we get to the crowd in the city above. You'll be okay."

Scout looked at Trevor. Trevor was looking up at her with bright blue eyes, his mittened hand out, waiting for her to take it and step on board.

She could hear the buzzing of the loudspeaker and the chimes that announced the doors were about to close.

She had to make a decision. She was out of time.

Emma started to take a step forward, to step off the tram, but Scout shook her head, stepping further back.

"No," Scout said. "It's better if I stay here. I don't want to bring trouble to you. You should go up to the city."

Scout expected Emma to try to argue, maybe even to jump off the tram and stay with Scout, but she just gave a curt nod.

"Okay," Emma said as she stepped back from the edge of the tramcar, away from the path of the door. "The code for our cabin is seven-seven-eight-seven. You can wait out the storm there; it's safer than yours. The communications will probably go down, but don't worry. We'll get back in touch with you as soon as we can. I hope you're wrong about the trouble, but I can see there's no arguing with you. I've been married to a marshal for far too long not to know what that tense set of the jaw means. Be safe, Scout."

Scott wanted to answer, but before she could get a word out, the doors slammed shut with a hiss, and the sound of the murmuring townspeople behind Emma and her family was cut off. Scout took another step back and watched the tram lift up into the sky.

The feeling of being watched had faded away. Scout almost hated that. Now she just felt alone.

Scout turned back to her dogs. If there were people lurking about, the dogs would flush them out. And they knew how to take care of themselves. They were both fast runners, although Gert was more inclined to fight than flee if Scout or Shadow were in danger.

Scout looked up at the sky. There was no sign of a cloud anywhere. Not of a storm cloud, anyway. The sky was never blue here, just hazy white, but it didn't look like anything dark or threatening was about to happen.

Not that she doubted that a storm was coming. Not after the whole town had promptly evacuated. It just bothered her that she might not have any warning of when it was about to strike. The rules here were apparently quite different from what she was used to. On the prairies of Amatheon, storms were visible for a long time before they were upon her. But with the mountains all around her, she could only see the sky directly above her, not all the way to a distant horizon.

The dogs were following a smell back down the snowy trench, and Scout trailed after, checking her pockets and making a mental inventory. Her marshal belt was around her waist, but it was under a coat that fell to her knees. Not easy to get to. She would have to adjust it before she ventured out next time.

Her slingshot and stones were in her coat pockets. She wasn't sure how it would work, trying to fire with mittens on. She hoped it wouldn't come up. She just had to get to the McGillicuddy cabin and turn on her AI and have Warrior help her turn it into the fortress Emma said it was.

That prickly feeling again. The moment she felt it, both dogs lifted their heads, smelling the air rather than the snowy path.

The village around them looked completely abandoned, but Scout was certain it was not. And looking around for hiding places wasn't going to reveal anything to her now that it hadn't revealed before.

She had to get back to the cabin.

Scout broke into a run, scooping Shadow up in her arms and whistling for Gert to follow. Gert charged on ahead, sending great plumes of powdery snow into the air.

Scout heard a whisper of air just by her ear, almost completely muffled by the thickness of her hat, but not quite. Then she saw a flash of red, the tail end of a dart burying itself into the snow.

Shi Jian had trained her assassins well. They never missed. Scout was being driven again, back to the cabin for some reason she couldn't even fathom.

And she was getting a sick feeling in her stomach that the sensation of being watched, the one that had convinced her not to step onto the tram, had been some deliberate manipulation on their part. They had revealed themselves just enough to set her on edge, to make her change her mind about leaving.

Gert had reached the fissure in the rock face and was galloping up the crude steps. The moment snow became bare rock, Scout dropped Shadow and spun around, slingshot at the ready. She pulled a mitten off with her teeth, leaving it to dangle from its cord at the end of her sleeve, then fit a stone into the sling's cup.

But she saw nothing. The village looked like it was hunkering down under the white blanket of the previous night's snow, waiting for the next covering to begin.

She retreated up the steps, pushing back her hood and hat to widen her field of view. She saw nothing, which was maddening, because her gut was certain they were closing in on her. Could they somehow swim through snow like fish in water without disturbing the surface?

Then Gert barked her fearsome hellhound bark, and Shadow yelped in a way Scout really didn't like. She turned to run up the last few steps to the plateau.

The cabin was there on the far side, glowing in the light from the sun rising behind Scout's back, like a shining goal she had almost reached. Just a few steps farther.

But those few steps were thick with kids in white jumpsuits and dully reflective masks under thick white hoods. She couldn't tell girls from boys, not with the masks covering their entire faces.

There were more than a dozen emerging from hiding places deep in the snow of the plateau. Four of them were attempting to stuff the dogs into sacks. Scout took half a step towards those four, but before she could even follow through on the motion, the others all charged at her, weapons raised.

But silent, so creepily silent.

Scout fired her slingshot, again and again. She made sure to hit the four trying to hurt her dogs, and Gert and Shadow were able to scurry out of anyone's reach, but they couldn't get to Scout, and she couldn't get to them.

And then the nearest two were on top of her–literally, as they tackled her to the ground, burying her in the snow. She kept a firm hold on her slingshot, but at such close range, it was all but useless.

Hands reached for her throat and, with a surge of anger-fueled adrenaline, Scout twisted out of the way. She was not going to be choked again. She threw back an elbow and heard a hiss of pain as one of the pairs of hands stopped grasping at her.

But it was quickly replaced by two other pairs. Someone caught her foot and pulled, sending Scout sprawling. Her face hit the frozen ground hard enough to make her nose crunch loudly, and she felt the hot wetness of her own blood running down her face.

Shadow yelped again, more in concern than pain, but it was still enough to give Scout another burst of anger. She lunged to her feet, sending a wave of snow up into the air. She couldn't get a rock out of her pocket fast enough, but she used the butt of the slingshot to poke a particularly grabby assassin in the throat just under the mask, and they fell away.

But there were just too many of them. She was never going to reach the safety of the cabin.

Suddenly the air was full of red darts. Scout ducked, covering her head with her arms, and waited for the needlelike sting of their strikes.

But the sting didn't come.

The dogs were barking again, excitedly. Scout lowered her arms to see the snow between her and the cabin strewn with fallen assassins. A few twitched their fingers or feet, but none of them could move well enough to get up out of the snow.

Paralyzed. Probably not permanently, though. Scout wouldn't be that lucky.

Shadow was still barking his relentless warning bark, and Scout looked up from the sprawled bodies of her enemies to the cabin on the far side of the plateau.

Someone was standing there. Someone in a white jumpsuit with a hood, looking just like the assassins but with goggles and a scarf covering their face instead of a mask, and with a billowing gray coat that floated like a cape behind them as they crossed the snowy field to where Scout stood speechless.

There was no reason to ask if they had done this. There was no sign of a dart gun or any other weapon in their gloved hands, but it was clear all the same. Nothing else could explain that sudden change in events.

"Who are you?" Scout asked instead.

The figure stopped a few meters away and reached up to push back the hood of the coat, then peeled away the glittering goggles that covered the top half of their face.

The goggles that had been protecting a pair of blue-gray eyes. A very familiar pair of blue-gray eyes. And the face? She knew that face as well.

Clementine.

It made no sense, but Scout could try to make sense of things later.

For now, the only thing to do was run.

10

SCOUT STUMBLED back into the fissure, nearly falling down the crude staircase but catching herself with her unmittened hand. The jutting rock was sharp, and she could see the blood welling up from under her palm, but the cold was so intense she couldn't feel it.

Yet.

Shadow collided with the back of her leg but quickly righted himself and charged on ahead, Gert close at his heels. Scout squeezed her bleeding, half-frozen hand tight and ran after.

At the bottom of the fissure, she chanced a look back. Clementine—or the Clementine doppelgänger or whoever they were—wasn't pursuing.

Scout didn't find that comforting.

The rising sun was warming the snow now, melting the top layer into a thick slush that clung to Scout's boots and slowed her steps. The dogs were having an even harder time. Shadow repeatedly got bogged down and had to put all of his energy into a super jump to get clear. Gert charged on like a tank, oblivious to the growing layer of the stuff clinging to her vest and dark fur.

Scout didn't like having Gert so far ahead of her. She hadn't counted heads up on the plateau, but there had been about a dozen, nowhere near the number of kids she had seen in the training room back on Bo Tajaki's ship. There must be others about, somewhere.

Even one waiting in the village to spring a trap on her was too many.

Scout didn't dare whistle for Gert to stop. Even the plastic dog whistle in her bag was no good; she had used it to cripple the assassins with their augmented hearing once before, but she knew they had compensated for that now. She would only give away her position.

But Gert didn't keep running all the way into town. When she reached the end of the trench, she turned to look back at Scout and Shadow. The wet snow gave way under her weight, spilling her into the trench, but her head quickly bounced up again as she waited for her companions to catch up.

Scout leaped down into the trench, then looked back again. Nothing. What did that mean?

Why had Clementine, or whoever, taken out all of Scout's attackers, then let Scout just run away?

Scout bent low and crept along the trench, searching for signs of other assassins lurking in the abandoned village.

She didn't have to search for long. There were another dozen of them on the tramway platform.

Scout squatted low, putting a hand on each of the dogs. Shadow jerked and looked back to see what was dripping on his back, and Scout realized she was still bleeding. She grabbed and squeezed a fistful of snow, hoping the cold would stop the flow.

She didn't know anything about living in the cold. But at least the numbness that came with it took the sting out of the cut on her palm. She would take it.

Scout watched the distant figures of the kids in white jumpsuits and face masks moving from pillar to pillar. Scout looked up the other way, following the wires up to the city on the mountaintop above. The last tram had disappeared. Scout couldn't make out any details at this distance, but she thought she saw where the wires ended: just above a pair of metal doors covering the opening in the stone wall.

At least the villagers were safe. And Emma and the boys.

Now Scout just had to find a way to safety herself.

When she had run back this way, she hadn't really had a plan, just a vague hope that she could find a way to call for another tram car to come get her. That hope swelled as she saw the kids stepping off the platform, disappearing among the cabins. Even white jumpsuits shouldn't be that hard to distinguish from snow; Scout suspected some sort of technology helping them disappear.

Still, she was certain none of them remained in the tram station. She would just wait a few minutes to be sure, then slip inside and see if she could make that call.

If that didn't work, she could try using the unlocking tool in her marshal belt on one of the cabins…

The thought was blown from her mind by a boom of noise, the boom that came just a fraction of a second after the shock wave bowled her over.

Scout gasped for breath, her diaphragm spasming painfully. Her ears were ringing, and white stars were exploding in front of her eyes.

It wasn't like she hadn't been knocked over by explosions before. Or by the destruction of her entire city. She even felt like she was bleeding from shallow cuts all over her body again, like that day when the shards of the dome that had failed to protect her family and her home had showered all over her and Shadow kilometers away across the prairie.

But it wasn't glass. It was snow, propelled by the explosion of the assassins destroying the tram station. Sharp ice, but not sharp enough to really cut her or her dogs.

Scout finally drew a proper breath, then sat up to look around.

No sign of the assassin kids. It was as if they had actually melted away.

Nothing remained of the station but a smoking crater and a wide blast pattern of soot and debris marring the drifts of snow. The cables had fallen to the ground of the steep mountainside.

Someone up top was bound to notice that. Someone official, someone who would want to fly down and investigate. She should stay nearby.

Scout unzipped her jacket, sucking her breath in with a loud hiss as the cold air quickly infiltrated her shirts and vest to freeze her skin. She retrieved the tool she needed from its pouch and rezipped her jacket, but it was like sealing that bubble of cold up with her. It was going to take a while for her body temperature to warm the inside of her jacket back up to something tolerable.

But the plan was to get inside a building. She wouldn't freeze before she accomplished that.

Scout touched each of the dogs to get their attention, then climbed up out of the trench to crawl over the snow to the nearest cabin. Shadow figured out what she was after and ran ahead, but Gert stayed at her side.

Scout would find that loyalty more admirable if Gert weren't a big black target against the white snow, slowly tracking alongside Scout. Just in case anyone on a rooftop wanted to snipe her.

Scout pushed herself to her feet and ran to the door. She put the device on the door and waited for the light on the side to turn green, to hear the little click of the locking mechanism inside the door opening up in the name of a galactic marshal.

Nothing happened. The red light on the tool flashed over and over as if wondering why its attempts to open the door weren't working.

Scout thrust the tool back into her pocket and looked around for signs of movement before risking the run to the next cabin.

That door wouldn't open either.

Scout put the tool back in her pocket, then struggled to pull her mitten back over her stiff hand. The bleeding had stopped, but so had any sense of feeling. That probably wasn't good. But the mittens felt unnaturally warm, like they had little heaters in them.

Or she was starting to lose it. Which might be more likely.

Shadow sniffed the air and Scout watched for what he would do next, but he apparently decided it was nothing and turned back to nose at Gert. He kept lifting his paws, one after the other, trying sometimes to keep two up at once.

Up out of the snow. He was going to freeze if she didn't get him to shelter.

Gert's wide paws seemed unbothered by the cold, but Scout had seen Gert ram things with her head and seem unstunned as well. It was possible she just wasn't smart enough to understand her own sensory input.

Scout bit her lip and looked around again, hoping for a sign. Perhaps a cabin with an inviting light that indicated its door still functioned or someone had left a back door open.

But all she noticed was that the light was getting darker, and thick flakes were starting to swirl down from the sky. Not many, and the paths they traced were beyond lazy, catching updrafts to dance back up before resuming their gentle fall.

But Scout wasn't fooled. The storm was starting. The one so severe that no one in town had elected to stay and weather it out.

She couldn't stay where she was, and she couldn't get back up the mountain. There was only one place to go.

Scout picked up Shadow, squeezing his little paws in the palms of her warm mittens, then clicked her tongue for Gert to follow her back up the trench.

By the time they reached the fissure, the lazy flakes in the air were so thick she couldn't see to the top of the stairs.

By the time she reached the top and stepped out onto the plateau, the wind had picked up as well. It still had no real strength to it, but it was filled with a blinding amount of snow and liked to blast it all right into Scout's face.

She didn't want to be blind here. Not here, on a field of snow strewn with enemies she knew were only temporarily paralyzed. They might recover at any moment. They wouldn't even have to regain use of all of their limbs. They could just reach out with their arms to trip her up and bring her down to their level.

She didn't like that image.

Scout hugged Shadow tighter, made sure Gert was still close at her heels, and pressed on. And tried really hard not to regret not getting on that tram. For all she knew, blowing the bottom tram station was only a last resort after she failed to show at the top. She might still have made the right choice, but she would never know for sure.

She couldn't see the cabin in front of her, was not even sure she hadn't veered too far in one direction or the other and was going to walk right past it. Worse, she was fairly certain she had forgotten the code to get inside. 7887? Or 7877? Would it give her a couple of tries, or would it lock her out entirely when she guessed wrong?

Would the door-opening tool be as ineffective here as it had been in the village?

Suddenly, a bright rectangle of light appeared ahead of her and a bit off to the right. She assumed it was a rectangle; the whirls of snow made the edges irregular, but she didn't know what it could be besides the open door of the cabin.

She was being lured in again. But Shadow in her arms was trembling despite the warmth of his own vest and her mittens on his feet. She had to get him inside. She shifted him a bit to get a rock in her hand, but that was the only preparation she could make for a fight.

She doubted it would be enough. She didn't dare hope the light was as inviting as it looked.

As she drew nearer, Scout could see the inside of the coatroom, now bereft of coats, although a dropped scarf lay twisted across the floor like a snake in motion, as if it had tried to follow the departing family.

No sign of a gray coat. No sign of anyone inside. Had the house recognized her when she approached?

It was a nice thought, but she didn't really believe it.

Scout waited for Gert to follow her into the coat room before shutting the door and putting Shadow down on the floor. It was warmer than outside, but not by much. Still, she pushed back her hood and goggles and lowered her scarf, then peeled off her mittens. Now, with both hands free, she could take out her slingshot before opening the inner door.

The kitchen was as they had left it, clean dishes now standing dry next to the sink, the honeypot still on the table. Scout stepped further into the room and looked the other way, towards the desk in its nook and the couch and chairs beyond.

Empty. Shadow sniffed the air, then Gert sniffed too. With the thick vests on, Scout couldn't see if the hair on their backs was rising up, but neither dog was growling or barking. Maybe they really were alone.

Scout crossed the living area to the short hallway that led to the cabin's two bedrooms. The boys' room was a mess of discarded items from the hasty packing of bags.

Then Scout heard the soft thump of a drawer closing in the McGillicuddys' room. She raised the slingshot, stone loaded and ready to fire before she stepped into the doorway.

The girl inside stood with her back to the door. Her goggles were dangling around her neck, and she had pushed back the tight-fitting hood of the jumpsuit. Her hair was darker than Scout remembered and cut so short it stood up on top of her head like a soft brush, nothing much like the long blonde locks from before.

Scout took careful aim at the back of her head. She knew from bitter experience that she would only get one shot at this.

"Before you do that, I should tell you one thing," the girl said without turning.

"What?" Scout demanded, not lowering her slingshot.

"I'm not Clementine."

11

SLOWLY, the girl turned around, hands raised in a nonthreatening gesture. The blue-gray eyes were the same, exactly the same. The times Clementine had leaned menacingly close to Scout's face when Scout had been tied to a chair or pinned under Clementine's unnaturally heavy body, there was no way she could ever forget those eyes.

And yet, the face wasn't quite right. This one looked both older and yet softer, the cheeks rounder with more color, the arch of her brown eyebrows a friendlier curve.

A sister? It was the only thing that made sense. But it was no comfort to Scout. Clearly, this girl was as resourceful and potentially as dangerous as her sister, perhaps more so since Clementine must have been the younger of the two. This girl was closer to Scout's age. A girl could learn a lot more ways to be deadly in four years.

What would she do if she knew what Scout had done to Clementine? Scout hadn't wanted to kill anybody. Not even after she had watched the twelve-year-old Clementine stab the galactic marshal Gertrude Bauer, the woman Scout had come to know under the name Warrior. Even then, Scout had only wanted to escape, but the ongoing solar storm had made that impossible.

And killing Clementine had been the only way to save her dog, Gert. There had been no other choice.

But she doubted Clementine's sister would see it that way.

What was her sister doing on Schneeheim, anyway? Why was she taking out other assassins for Scout's benefit? It made no sense.

Scout was still standing in the doorway, slingshot raised but arms starting to tremble from the effort of keeping it drawn and ready to fire. Her dogs, finished with whatever they had been exploring in the kitchen, came up behind her to sniff at the bedrooms.

Shadow was distracted by the plethora of boy smells from the room across the hall, but Gert came right up beside Scout. The vest she wore made it impossible to see if her hackles were raised in that fearsome way that made her look so intimidating, but she was growling a low warning that was almost subsonic, and Scout knew that meant Gert was in full hellhound mode.

Scout lowered her weapon to quickly touch her palm to the top of Gert's head, hoping to calm her.

She was afraid of what this girl might do if the dog attacked her.

Then a different sort of low roar grew louder than Gert's growl. Scout frowned, not sure what she was hearing, but the girl's face transitioned from a careful projection of her lack of harmful intent to high alert in one blink of her wide eyes.

"They're coming," she said. She brushed past Scout and Gert in the doorway without a second glance, only touching the back of her hand to Scout's shoulder to move her to one side, but even that little gesture sent Scout stumbling into the doorframe.

"Hey," Scout said as she regained her balance and followed the girl back to the living room. "We weren't done talking."

"No more time," the girl said, touching the screen on the desk in its little nook. Scout didn't know how she had done it, but the screen was filled with little boxes showing different angles of the storm outside. A few showed lights dancing in the distance.

"Your friends?" Scout asked.

"No more than yours," the girl said, again moving Scout to one side so she could get at the couch in the far corner of the room. Two backpacks were waiting there, the exact same packs Scout had seen on the assassins. The girl thrust one into Scout's arms, then pulled the other onto her own back.

"Where did you get this?" Scout asked.

"From the fallen," the girl said before settling her goggles over her eyes and wrapping her scarf around the rest of her face. "Hurry!" she said again, voice muffled but urgency clear.

"Where can we go in this storm?" Scout asked. "None of the other cabins will open up." But even as she said it, she was pulling the pack onto her back. This girl seemed to have a plan, which was more than Scout had. And she knew they had to get out of here. Those lights must have been attached to vehicles.

There had been a lot of lights.

The girl charged out both of the cabin doors, out into the thickening swirl of falling snow. Scout pulled the doors shut after she and the dogs were both through. The outer door made a heavy clanking sound when she closed it, and something inside beeped a single warning beep.

Scout had to jog to catch up with the girl, stopping to pick up Shadow, who had quickly realized the snow was just as cold as ever. Gert stayed close to Scout, but she never stopped growling.

The girl led the way up to the higher cliff where the other cabin stood, but she shied away from it, finding another path that led them up to an even higher cliff that overlooked both of the other two plateaus.

She didn't bother trying to hide, just walked straight up to the edge to look down. Scout stayed further back. She could see the lights converging on the McGillicuddy cabin. It wouldn't take them long to realize she wasn't there, to start looking around.

"Get down!" Scout hissed at the girl, who ignored her. The edges of her gray coat snapped in the air so loudly Scout was certain the assassins below would hear it just as soon as they cut off their engines.

Scout hugged Shadow tighter, squatting to put an arm around the still-growling Gert as well. Gert paused in her growl to nestle closer to Scout's warmth, but her eyes never left the new girl.

"What are we waiting for?" Scout asked, but the girl didn't answer, just watched as the others below circled the cabin, failed to break in through the front door, then gathered in a huddle to discuss what to do.

"We should go," Scout said, and when the girl still didn't answer, Scout rose to her feet to start hunting for another path to a higher cliff, perhaps one more out of the wind. But the girl, without turning around, extended a hand behind her in a sign that Scout and the dogs should stay where they were.

The assassins were circling around the cabin again. This time, when they gathered in a huddle some distance away, it wasn't to whisper together. There was a bright flash of light, a pillar of flash fire rising up into the sky before quickly dying out in the thin air.

When the smoke cleared, Scout saw the entire exterior of the cabin was blackened, bits around the door looking almost melted like wax.

If she had been inside, she would have survived that explosion just fine. And she doubted they had any bigger tricks in their bags to bust inside; she would have been safe.

But that door was impassable now. She had chosen to leave the cabin. Even after Emma had told her how safe it was. All because a girl with no name had told her to?

Scout resisted the urge to beat herself up too much. It wasn't the time for it. But she needed to figure out how to keep moving forward on the path she had chosen.

"Let's go," the girl said, finally turning back to Scout and the dogs.

"No," Scout said, setting Shadow down so she could straighten to her full height with her arms crossed. This girl had to see she meant business.

"What do you mean, no? You've been hissing at me to get going since we got outside."

"Not until you tell me who you are," Scout said.

"You know who I am," the girl said.

"I know you're like them," Scout said, jerking her head towards the plateau below where the assassins were still in a huddled meeting. "I know you're one of them."

"Never," the girl said venomously.

"You're not Clementine, but you're like Clementine," Scout said.

"It's complicated. Very complicated. We don't have the time," the girl said. There was an edge to her voice that wasn't exactly panic, but her sense of urgency was overwhelming her attempts at being conciliatory.

"I've been led about more than once," Scout said. "That crew has gotten me just where they want me. For all I know, being on this entire planet was all part of the plan. So how do I know you're not just another, more involved, part of the same trap?"

"I saved you," the girl said, gesturing at the snowy field below, still strewn with paralyzed kids. Some of the newer arrivals were digging them out of the snow, lifting them up onto the backs of the vehicles.

"That could have been part of the plan," Scout said. "You dress like them. You behave like you've had the same training as them. You have the same equipment, and I don't just mean the packs. You took those kids down with darts."

"Nonlethal darts," the girl said. "And an older model than they're packing."

"You left them to get buried in the snow outside an abandoned village," Scout said, feeling her anger rising. "How is that nonlethal?"

"You know them!" the girl said, flinging her hands up in frustration. "You know how hard they are to kill! But what are you accusing me of? Killing them or being on their side?"

"It doesn't matter," Scout said. "I just know I can't trust you."

"You have to trust me," the girl said.

They both had more to say, but Gert's growling suddenly kicked up from that low menace to a teeth-baring snarl, and Scout realized with a start that the dog had left her side, had advanced so far that the girl no longer had a way to get off the jutting rock she had stepped out on to look below.

No way except through Gert, and Gert wasn't going to back off.

"Don't hurt her," Scout said. "I can call her off. I think."

The girl scoffed at Scout, and Scout was afraid she was going to charge the dog, perhaps just to prove she could.

But she didn't. She changed her posture, letting the anger melt out of her tense limbs and turning sideways, so her silhouette was smaller.

"Hey, girly-girl," she said softly, not looking Gert straight in the eye.

Gert's snarl settled back into the warning growl, but her own posture was still tense.

Scout started to step forward, to make a grab for Gert's collar, but the girl glared up at her and shook her head. Then she turned her attention back to the dog, advancing slowly, not directly towards her but off to one side.

"It's okay, girly-girl," she all but cooed, peeling off a glove to present one bare hand for the dog to sniff.

Gert held her ground, but when the hand drew close enough, she sniffed it, one quick sniff as if she were determined not to be impressed.

Then, to Scout's surprise, she sat down in the snow, tail thumping as she looked up at the girl so like that other girl who not so many days ago had tried to kill her.

Scout guessed Gert didn't hold a grudge. Or this girl smelled very different from her sister.

"Good girly-girl," the girl said, scratching at the dog's ears.

"Her name is Gert," Scout said.

"I know," the girl said. Then she pulled her glove back on and walked up to Scout. "I'm Daisy. And I know your trust is going to be harder to earn than Gert's. I'm prepared for that. But if we don't get higher up this mountain, I'm never going to get that chance. Let's go."

She didn't wait for Scout to voice a decision, just started up a narrow trail Scout could barely even make out under the deep layers of snow. Shadow went trotting after her, Gert bounding to catch up.

Scout hoped her dogs' instincts were right. But even if this Daisy were someone to be trusted, it would take a unique sort of person not to have pretty strong feelings about the person who killed her own sister.

If she had any other choice, she would take it, but she didn't. Scout hoisted the pack higher up on her shoulders and followed her dogs.

12

THE PATH GREW STEEPER the higher they climbed, and Scout doubted she would even know where to step if Daisy with her heavily augmented body weren't blazing the trail. Gert was widening her bit of it enough for Shadow to follow delicately behind her, only occasionally getting buried under a loose drift that fell like a mini-landslide down the side of the rock face on either side of the trail.

At last, the path emerged from the fissure in the rock, ending on a much narrower cliff than the last one. Scout stayed close to the rock face that loomed ahead of them, but Daisy stepped out further to get a look below.

"What's going on?" Scout asked, not wanting to venture out to look herself. She wasn't afraid of heights, not after being tossed off a platform on *Amatheon Orbiter 1* and surviving, but she wasn't sure she knew enough about how snow behaved besides being cold, wet, and slippery.

She didn't want to try combining the last of those qualities with the edge of a steep drop-off.

"They're leaving the cabin," Daisy said.

"Going back to town?" Scout asked.

"No, breaking into groups to follow us."

"So they didn't find our tracks?" Scout asked, but the quick shake of Daisy's head killed her burgeoning hope.

"No, they did," Daisy said. "They're sending smaller groups out on other trails to see if they can cut us off, outflank us, find a good position for an ambush or long-range sniping—"

"I've got it," Scout said. She didn't need more stuff to worry about that she didn't know how to defend against, although she guessed it was good that Daisy was listing it all inside her own head.

"Let's press on," Daisy said, stepping back from the cliff and looking around before choosing the next path further up.

"Press on to where?" Scout asked.

Daisy blinked. "I thought that was obvious. To the city."

"We'll be safe there?" Scout asked.

"No," Daisy said, looking even more confused. "Shi Jian is there."

"Oh," Scout said.

If Shi Jian were there, Scout would rather be anywhere else.

But the Torreses and the McGillicuddys were also up there. If Shi Jian couldn't get her hands on Scout, she might harm them instead.

Or they could also be on her hit list, being tangled up in the Tajaki trade dynasty court case just as much as Scout was.

"Do you know how to get there?" Scout asked as Daisy continued surveilling the options from the cliff they were huddled on.

"Up," Daisy said.

"No, I mean, you seem to know where trails are," Scout said.

"We're not on trails," Daisy said. "No one is crazy enough to walk up this mountain. But I studied the slope from above before I came down to the village. It's climbable without gear. We'll be fine."

"We can't get up there before dark," Scout said. "It's too far."

"Way too far," Daisy agreed. "We'll be lucky to make it before dark tomorrow night. Probably won't."

"We can't climb in the dark," Scout said.

Daisy leaned closer to peer at Scout's eyes through the reflective surface of her goggles. "Get your glasses on under those," she ordered. "They have night vision."

"Oh, yes," Scout said, patting her pockets until she found her round-lensed glasses. She pulled off her goggles and hat, her entire body shivering instantly and intensely at the kiss of cold against the exposed skin of her head and neck. She pulled the frames around her ears and slammed the hat back down. Daisy helped her get the goggles settled over the glasses.

"Night vision," Scout said, trying to sound casual. Warrior was the one who told her how to use technology, but Scout was reluctant to turn her on now. Daisy had all the augments Clementine had had, maybe more. She would see Warrior the moment she appeared. It might be important later that Daisy didn't know Scout had an AI with her.

But the glasses responded to her command and just like she had been able to see the walls on the tribunal enforcers' ship, everything here shifted to green tones, the lines of the world around her suddenly sharply defined.

"Wow," Scout said, looking around. "I hadn't realized it had already gotten so dark. The days are short here."

"Part of that is the storm," Daisy told her. "But your glasses filter out the snowflakes so you can see the ground better. Try looking at a distance."

Scout looked around, then crept just a bit closer to the edge of the cliff to look down.

Not only could she see every detail of the still-smoldering cabin on the plateau and the smaller one huddled above it; she could see every cabin in the village around the remains of the tramway platform. She could even tell where the doors were by the pinpricks of light that shone down on their stoops.

"Amazing," Scout said, then felt her cheeks flush at how silly she sounded. Daisy had spent her whole life around far more impressive technology. Luckily, the layers of her scarf concealed her embarrassment.

"This looks like the best option," Daisy said, looking up another fissure through a rock face. "The others would be too steep for the dogs. At some point, we might end up carrying them, but they should pull their own weight as long as they're able."

Scout, who had once crossed a prairie with Gert on her back and Shadow in her arms, couldn't argue with that. The dogs got heavy fast.

It was slow going, making sure each step was secure before putting their full weight on it, then moving the other foot and finding a grip on the rock under the loose snow. Gert seemed indefatigable, plowing through what little Daisy left behind. Shadow wasn't happy about how cold any of it was but seemed to appreciate that it would be much worse without the two ahead of him getting the worst of it out of his way.

Scout brought up the rear, partly because Daisy was better at finding and creating their trail, but mostly because she wanted her dogs in front of her, where she could always see them.

She ignored the prickly feeling on the back of her neck, that feeling of being followed. They had a big head start on the assassins, and the snow was falling more and more thickly as the day drew on, covering their trail behind them. She doubted they'd lose the assassins entirely, but there were a lot of places where they might choose the wrong path and have to backtrack.

Or so Scout hoped. All she knew was when she looked back, she saw no signs of pursuit.

But the climb was tiring. Scout was bathed in sweat under the layers of warm clothing, and her heart was beating way too fast. She panted to keep up with the girl, but a tickle in her throat had her coughing again and again. Was she getting ill?

That didn't seem likely; they would have noticed it when doing her medical processing, surely. And yet, she didn't feel right. She had spent days on end under the hot prairie sun pedaling up steep hillsides. She had never tired this quickly.

Another tickle of cough grew into a fit that forced her to stop climbing for a moment. When she at last had her breath back, she looked up to find she was quite alone. No sign of Daisy, no sign of her dogs.

They couldn't have gotten too far away from her, but when Scout lifted her foot to take another step, she suddenly got very confused about where she was going. They were in less of a fissure at this point than a narrow runnel, and the runnel branched and branched again.

Scout could see the indents forming over the top of the snow that showed where the runnels were, but they were all disturbed, as if Daisy and the dogs had split up and plowed through everything.

Where had they gone?

Scout took another step forward but neglected to be sure of her footing before putting her weight forward, and her boot skidded off the rock face. She went down on one knee, hard. Her thick layers of clothing, the ones she was sweating like mad under, protected her kneecap from the worst of it, but she still had tears in her eyes.

She sat down in the snow, rubbing at her knee as she looked up the slope again. Where had they gone? Her dogs never lost sight of her if they could help it.

Had Daisy abducted them somehow? That didn't seem likely, but Scout's thoughts were a muddle.

She just needed a little rest, and then she could find her dogs. But even sitting still, she couldn't slow her breath or her heartbeat. The frozen chill of the rock beneath her was penetrating her coat and pants, seeping into her bones, and her sweat-soaked inner clothing was clinging to her now-goosefleshed skin.

She started to shiver. And once she started, she couldn't stop.

Somewhere in the back of her head, she knew she should get up and get moving, but her muddled brain decided against it. She didn't know which of the paths Daisy and the dogs had chosen. Perhaps the best thing would be to wait for them to circle back for her. To get her heart rate down to a place where it wasn't beating so loudly in her ears.

She tucked her mittened hands into her armpits, hugging herself close as she waited.

Her rapid breathing began to slow to a hypnotic pace, and her eyelids grew heavier and heavier.

She thought she heard something over the wind, someone calling her name. But was it Daisy or the assassins in pursuit, trying to trick her into revealing herself? Better to remain silent. Daisy knew how to find her.

She did wish she had her dogs beside her, though. The dogs always knew how to warm her.

Although maybe she didn't need that anymore either, because she felt suddenly, strangely warm all over, like a cloud of magical warmth had settled down over her, a gift from the sky. It hugged her like an ephemeral blanket, so cozy.

Her bone-shaking shivers finally stopped.

She was so very warm.

13

SCOUT SAT UP, heart racing. But this wasn't the thready, ineffectual fast beat from before. No, this time it was a strong, hard beat pounding alertness to every bit of her body. She could see the world around her in sharp detail, hear every skitter of a snowflake hitting the rock face around her, process sensory detail from every distinct nerve ending over her entire body.

Or at least it felt that way. It was all too much. She wanted to scream, but a hand was already pressed tight across her mouth to hold the sound in.

"Easy," Daisy said. "Give it a minute. The first jolt is the worst."

Scout took a few deep breaths through her nose, and as she willfully forced the tension out of her body, Daisy dropped her hand. Scout took a few more breaths before asking, "First jolt of what?"

"Stim," Daisy said, putting a little injector back into her coat pocket. "You needed it."

"Something's wrong," Scout said. Her crystal-clear vision was starting to swim again, and she rubbed at her goggles.

"I guessed that," Daisy said. "Hold still; I need to check something."

Scout flinched back, but the device in Daisy's gloved hand wasn't another injector or needle, just a small scanner. She passed it over Scout's arms and chest and peered closely at the screen.

"Am I dying?" Scout asked, only half joking. The stim was still trying to make her heart pound, but the beats were getting weaker again, the urge to lie down and let sleep take her returning.

"Your nanite has been compromised," Daisy said, slipping the pack off her back and turning it around to search one of the side pockets. "The one that's supposed to help you deal with the low oxygen."

"How?" Scout asked.

"Either it was defective when it was injected into you, or someone gave you a counteragent after the fact," Daisy said, finding what she was searching for: a metal box. She flipped open the lid, and Scout saw another injector nestled within, smaller than the one the doctor had injected her with, but of a similar design. Daisy looked at a few of the vials nestled in the foam that filled the lid, then selected one and slipped it into the bottom of the injector handle.

"I'm not getting enough oxygen?" Scout said.

"Correct," Daisy said, pushing back Scout's sleeve and pressing the injector to the inside of her wrist.

The little injector hurt more than the big one had. And the world around Scout was still swimming away.

"Here," Daisy said, and Scout realized she had dozed off again. She opened her eyes and let Daisy help her put a small mask over her nose and mouth. "Just breathe normally. By the time this tank is out, your nanite should be up to full strength."

"But what if I still have the counteragent in my system?" Scout asked, her voice muffled by the mask. Daisy used heavy-duty tape to attach the little oxygen tank to the side of Scout's pack.

"I'll check you in a few hours," Daisy said, putting the injector away and standing up to get her pack back on. "If you're right, I can just keep injecting you with nanites until we get to the city."

Scout looked around, her brain still fuzzy. Something was missing.

"The dogs!" she said when she finally worked out what it was.

"The dogs are fine," Daisy assured her. "I tied them up there so they wouldn't get in the way."

Scout looked up to the top of the flat slope of the rock face and saw

Shadow pressed close to Gert's side, shivering like mad. They both started bounding up and down when she looked their way.

"Have their nanites been compromised as well?" Scout asked.

"I don't think so. They don't show any signs, and they likely would have succumbed before you did, especially the little fellow. But I can check them when we get up there."

She held out a hand, and Scout took it to let her pull her to her feet. Scout got up and then dropped Daisy's hand, but was immediately overwhelmed by another wave of dizziness. She dropped her head, pressing her mittened hands to her temples as she willed the weakness to pass.

She heard three soft sounds, something—or things—landing softly in the mounds of snow nearby. Then Daisy was yelling a fearsome war cry.

Scout lifted her head from her hands and saw Daisy rushing over the slippery, steep slope of the rock face to meet their three attackers. She kept her body weight low and moved with inhuman speed, striking the first on the side of the knee with a quick kick, then catching the fist of the next one as they tried to take a jab at her and using the assassin's own momentum to throw it into the third, who had just been raising a dart gun to fire.

"Here!" Daisy shouted, and she threw something. Scout followed the glittering object's arc through the sky. Her vision was still strange, like she was watching a video that kept starting and stopping in a jerky manner rather than playing in a smooth progression. But she forced herself to focus, to follow the path and catch what Daisy had thrown to her.

A gun. But not a dart gun. This was a proper weapon, the kind the marshals carried.

Scout looked back up and saw Daisy trading blows with first one and then another of the assassins. She was good; she was pushing them back hard enough that they couldn't overwhelm her, but Scout didn't see how she could change her position from purely defensive to offensive.

She was going to get tired, and then they would have her.

Worse, the third had gotten back to their feet and was raising the dart gun once more.

"Scout!" Daisy shouted, but both of her foes rushing her at once drowned out the rest of her words.

Scout looked at the gun in her hands. She hated the things. What if it wasn't even linked to her as Gertrude Bauer's had been? But surely Daisy wouldn't have tossed her a weapon she couldn't fire.

The third assassin lowered the dart gun, unable to get a clear shot, and ran forward to join the fistfight. Scout raised the gun and tried to aim.

Her brain still felt fuzzy, and her hand was shaking. She brought up her other hand to brace it, but the barrel was still dancing around.

What if she hit Daisy? She and the dogs would really be lost then. And yet, Daisy had been at a standstill fighting just two assassins. She was never going to be able to take three.

"Scout!" Daisy shouted again, half a grunt as she put everything into a powerful kick that sent one of the assassins sprawling.

They wouldn't be down for long.

Scout made her way across the rock face as quickly as she could, which wasn't very fast. Walking across the slope was harder than climbing up a fissure, and her boots kept slipping on the slick, wet rock.

She reached the assassin just as they were getting back up, weight on the balls of their feet as they prepared to spring back into the fray. Scout swung the gun down with both hands as hard as she could, bringing the thick handle down on the back of the assassin's head. Its body crumpled at her feet.

Daisy was still caught between the other two, ducking and dodging so feverishly she didn't have an opening to land a blow of her own.

"Scout!" she cried again. Clearly, her patience was at an end. Scout tried aiming the gun again, but her hands were wobbling even worse than before.

If she shot Daisy...

Scout's vision blurred from tears of tired frustration, but with the glasses and goggles both on, there was no way to brush them aside. Instead, she blinked, hard, then reached into her pocket and found a stone. She didn't even bother with the slingshot, just flung it at the assassin, who was a little further away from Daisy than the other.

It hit the assassin's temple with a soft thud, and they fell to their knees, hands pressed to their head. Daisy wasted no time; as soon as their head was low enough, she kicked them hard. She wasn't even facing them—she was turned to take on the other one advancing on her—but her mule kick caught the assassin in the jaw, and their head snapped back.

They seemed to hang there, bent back, for a long, long moment. Then they fell to the snow.

With only one left to fight, Daisy made quick work of it. The last assassin was raining blows down at her at a pace too quick for Scout's eyes to even follow, but Daisy dodged them all easily, redirecting the momentum with a series of blocks.

Then, when she was close enough, she made a quick jab of her own. The assassin staggered back, their nose gushing what looked like far too much blood. Then Daisy hit them again, and they were down.

Daisy stood, fists still clenched, for several long minutes until her breath finally slowed back to normal. Then she went from body to body, gathering up their mittens and stuffing them into her own pockets.

Then she looked up at Scout, and Scout felt her cheeks flushing red with shame. Daisy didn't say anything, but she didn't need to. Scout knew she had let her down.

Scout held out the gun as if her mittened palms were a platter. Daisy snatched it up and stuffed it back into its holster, then adjusted the scarf that had fallen loose from around her face.

She looked up and frowned, and Scout looked up too. It was impossible to say where these three had dropped down from. There was nothing directly above them. Did they have some sort of silent flying vehicle?

But Daisy didn't seem to be worried about it. She climbed back up the rock face to where she had left the dogs and untied them, but held the leashes until Scout reached the top.

Then the dogs were all over her, trying to lick at her face despite the goggles and layers of wrapped scarf. Scout let them expend their energy and then looked up at Daisy, who had the scanner in her hand.

"They're fine," she said, and Scout could tell by the clipped sound of the words that she was still angry. "Let's go."

Scout nodded and got to her feet. Her head was clearer, although the plastic mask over her face was far from comfortable. Her breath was filling it with vapor, making a humid pocket of air that was far from pleasant to breathe through.

But she wasn't going to take it off until Daisy told her to. She was going to have to try harder to keep up with Daisy. It wouldn't be easy, not with all the augments Daisy's body had that Scout lacked.

But she had to do whatever she could to keep Daisy from asking any questions that would lead to grilling Scout about her aversion to guns.

Because that would just lead back to Clementine.

14

SCOUT KNEW the days were short, and the nights were long on this planet, at least currently. It made sense to keep plowing on despite the total darkness. She could see well enough with the night vision her glasses provided for her, even if the incessant green was starting to give her a headache.

But the dogs were having a tougher time. They stayed close by Scout, watching her for guidance. They both kept on going, putting one paw in front of another, but she could see they were tiring. They were letting more and more of the thick snow coat their backs before shaking it away.

Actually, the thick layer of snow was probably warming. With no exposed flesh, Scout only had a vague sense through the layers of her clothing that the temperature was dropping, but she knew that it was. And her dogs had only the vests to protect them, vests only really designed to keep them weighted down in the low gravity.

Daisy ranged farther and farther ahead, sometimes checking out multiple paths before coming back to get Scout and the dogs going on the better one before running forward again. She was like a machine, never tiring.

Scout still had stim running through her bloodstream, but she didn't like it. It made her teeth grind together and her muscles clench, and the light from her glasses was piercingly bright. And on top of all that, she was still tired.

Shadow stopped walking and lifted his paws with a little whine, one after another, then two at once. He even tried three, teetering on a single paw before falling into the snow.

Scout tried to urge him to keep moving, but he wouldn't budge. She dropped to one knee and took one of his paws in her mittened hand. The bottom was raw and bloody from walking over freezing rock and snow.

Scout unzipped her coat, her breath hissing at the sudden rush of cold, then bundled him inside to zip it back up around him. She still had to hold him up with her hands, but he would get warmer soon.

She could press on. She could keep up, even with the extra weight. She had to. It had been hours since they had been jumped by the last three assassins. They must have been missed by now. Their compatriots would be on top of them all too soon. She had to keep going.

Scout hugged Shadow close and took another step up the mountain, but this time it was Gert who made a soft whine and refused to take another step. Scout looked down at her. She wasn't lifting her paws as Shadow had done. It was almost like she wasn't sure why she was whining. But Scout could see the bloody paw prints up the trail behind her, little pools spreading out beneath her as she stood looking up at Scout with great sad eyes.

"What's the problem?" Daisy asked as she came jogging back down the path. "It's barely steep at all here. We should be making much better time."

"The dogs," Scout said. "I don't think they can keep walking like this over these trails. It's too tough on their feet. I can handle Shadow all right if you can carry Gert?"

Daisy's head tipped as she looked down at Gert. With her face wrapped in a scarf that even overlapped the edges of her goggles, it was impossible to see her face, but Scout could feel her frowning darkly at the three of them.

But then she turned and marched back up the hill without a word.

Was she leaving them behind?

"Come on, Gert," Scout said. "Can you walk a little?"

Gert wagged her tail gamely, but when Scout took a few steps, Gert remained behind.

Scout walked back to Gert's side and squatted down to press her scarf-covered face to Gert's, ignoring Shadow's grumble of protest at being crushed against her.

What was she going to do?

Then Daisy was back, gently moving Scout aside so she could scoop Gert up in her arms. She led the way back up the path, even with the extra weight moving faster than Scout could follow. By the time Scout caught up with her, they were in a small canyon deep in a rock fissure, out of the worst of the blinding storm. And, in a little niche in the rock off to one side, Daisy had erected some sort of tent-like shelter. Daisy was on her knees in the doorway, laying Gert inside. She held the door for Scout and Shadow to follow, then sealed it up behind them.

Was she still mad about the fight before? Or was she mad because they were stopping when she was clearly prepared to keep marching all night?

Scout heard a rustle of sound outside the structure and put a mittened hand against the canvas roof. She could feel it shiver as something slid over the top of it. Then there was another rustle, and a weight pressed against her hand.

Daisy was covering the shelter with snow. For warmth or for camouflage? Probably for both, Scout decided.

The sounds grew more and more muffled as the snow over the walls and ceiling grew thick. Then there was a different sort of sound, and Scout guessed that Daisy was digging with her hands through the snow, scooping and packing over and over.

The temperature inside the shelter rose to something almost like a comfortable level, and Scout unzipped her coat to let Shadow come out. He took a few shaky steps over the canvas floor, but the cold from the stone beneath the floor was still intense, and he quickly raced to Gert's side to curl up against her and get to the business of licking each of his paws, one after another.

And then each of Gert's, as she had fallen into an instant deep sleep and was not so fussy over wounds as Shadow was.

The door of the shelter shook, then Daisy found the opening and crawled inside, sealing it back up behind her. She slipped off her pack, and Scout realized she was still sitting with hers on.

It shouldn't have been so difficult to get the straps off her shoulders, but her brain still felt thick and stupid. Plus, she seemed to be tangled in something. Daisy caught her hands to stop her flailing about, then pulled off the oxygen bottle that had been taped to the side of her pack. She took the mask off Scout's face as well, dislodging most of her scarf in the process. The rush of cold air on Scout's skin woke her brain up a little, but only for a moment.

Scout was starting to realize that cold had a lot of degrees to it. And she had no idea just how much worse it got than what she'd already felt. She didn't want to know.

Mask and hose gone, Scout got back to work removing her pack. By the time she had it, Daisy had set up a little glowing thing in the middle of the tent. It was giving off both light and heat, and Scout regretted not finding the one in her pack and starting it up sooner. Then Daisy found two self-heating containers of soup and activated the heating elements. She handed one to Scout without a word.

Scout unwrapped her scarf, then pulled her mittens off with her teeth and just sat for a moment with the warm disposable cup in her hands, breathing in the aroma of chicken and thick egg noodles. The steam felt good on her cheeks, dissipating some of the numbness.

Daisy took off her scarf and goggles and then her hat, scratching at the short bristles of her brown hair with both hands until it all stood on end again. Then she picked up the soup and took a long pull, drinking down the broth before setting it aside. She chewed at the chicken and noodles in her mouth, cheeks bulging like a nut-hoarding rodent, as she reached into her coat pockets and took out the three pairs of mittens she had taken from the assassins that had jumped them on the rock face.

"Eat," she said to Scout after swallowing her overly large mouthful of food. "We have more food in the packs, but soup is the best to start. You need the energy."

Scout took off her goggles and hat, then sipped at the soup. It was saltier than Scout was used to, but the long, thick noodles were a treat.

Her stomach, as if suddenly realizing it hadn't been keeping her up to date on its empty status, growled loudly, and Scout took another swallow.

"About what happened down below," Daisy said, eyes on the mittens as she arranged them into some design on the canvas floor in front of her crossed legs.

"I'm sorry," Scout started to say, but Daisy waved that away.

"Apologies aren't going to help things," Daisy said. "Your nanite is working now, so low oxygen levels aren't going to be a problem. You've acclimated as well as can be expected to the low gravity, so that's not a factor either. But that's as far as my diagnosis goes."

"I don't understand," Scout said.

"I don't either," Daisy said, gesturing for Scout to finish her soup. She took another swallow of her own, then took another small pack out of her bag as she chewed. She turned one of the mittens over in her hand and started cutting at it with a small pair of scissors she produced from the little pack. Her eyes were on her work, not on Scout, as she said, "I need you to explain why you couldn't take the shot."

"I didn't have a shot to take," Scout said. "You'd just given me the stim. I wasn't quite recovered from passing out. My hands were shaking like crazy. I didn't have a clear shot at any of them that didn't risk hitting you."

Daisy said nothing, just kept turning and snipping at the mitten. She set it aside and took another gulp of soup before picking up the next one. "There's more to it than that," she said as she snipped.

Scout suspected she wasn't looking at her on purpose. Perhaps she thought that made it easier for Scout to talk. Maybe it did, but like the cold, it was a thing that had a lot of degrees far past the point where Scout was comfortable.

"I've been through some things," Scout said.

"So have I," Daisy said.

"I've had to do some things."

"So have I."

Scout bit her lip and focused her eyes on the empty cup in her hands. "I've done things I don't want to do, ever again. I felt like I had to at the time, but I don't feel good about it. And when I come close to having to do it again, I just can't."

Daisy drank the last of her soup, then set down the mitten to dig through her pack again. She tossed something in a plain brown wrapper to Scout, then sat down with another of the same in her hands. Scout peeled back the wrapper and found a stack of crackers with peanut butter smeared thickly between the layers. She took a bite, careful not to waste any crumbs by crumbling the crackers too much.

"If the moment comes again and you can't step up, we're lost," Daisy said. "I'm not here to rescue you, you know. I'm here because I need an ally. You have to be that. I can't do this on my own."

"Do what?" Scout asked. "Get up the mountain? I think you could."

"Getting up the mountain is only where this all starts," Daisy said. "I'm after Shi Jian. And given what she's done to you and yours, I assumed you were with me on that."

"I can't take her on," Scout said. "She's not even human."

"I'm not entirely human either. Not anymore," Daisy said bitterly. "Thanks to her."

"She modified you against your will?" Scout asked. It never occurred to her that the army of assassins hadn't volunteered. As much as one could meaningfully volunteer at that age.

"That's the least of what she did to me," Daisy said. "But that's not the main thing."

Scout took another bite of crackers and peanut butter. The dogs were both awake now, watching her intently. She broke off two large chunks, one for each of them, and they ate them eagerly.

"I don't see where I come into this," Scout said. "I'm not like you. I don't have augmentations. I'm not a fighter."

"You once wanted to join the rebellion, didn't you?" Daisy said.

"That was a long time ago," Scout said, wondering how Daisy even knew about that.

Or how much more she knew.

"You need to find that spirit again," Daisy said. "We have to stop Shi Jian. Before she kills you, which she fully intends to do."

"Why do you care if Shi Jian kills me?" Scout asked.

"I care about stopping everything Shi Jian wants to do. Because it's all bad, and it's bad on a level I don't think you even grasp. You realize the Tajaki trade dynasty is one of the most powerful families in the galaxy? And Shi Jian infiltrated them to manipulate them?"

"For some sort of financial gain? Or political power or something?" Scout guessed.

"That's just the thing," Daisy said, putting the scissors away and fishing around in the little box until she found a needle and a spool of shiny black thread. "I've been trying to get to the bottom of what she's up to for years now. *Years*. And as best as I can tell, she's doing this just for kicks."

"For kicks?" Scout repeated. "She put one of my friends in a coma she might never recover from, and it was just for kicks?"

"Yes," Daisy said with deadly seriousness. "But that's just because all of this that we know about? It's just a thing she's got going on on the side. She has a real mission, and I don't think she's acting alone. She's been inside the Tajaki trade dynasty for more than a decade, but I don't know why. Is she waiting for something? Some sort of signal or command?" She ended with a shrug.

"That's why her body augments are so advanced? Because she's working for someone even richer than the Tajaki trade dynasty?" Scout guessed.

"Yes," Daisy said, sounding happy that Scout was finally catching on. "So ask yourself, who would pay for such things? And what would they want in return?"

"I don't know," Scout said miserably. "Until a few days ago, I knew nothing about even life in orbit around my planet, let alone life in Galactic Central. I don't have a clue."

"But you're getting a sense of the scope," Daisy said. "Shi Jian is killing time with us, waiting for word from her employer. I really want to take her out before she gets that word. Because whatever it is that she's lying in wait like a sleeper agent to do, it just has to be bad. But even aside from that, all of this she's killing time doing is going to put your friends in danger. Mortal danger. And I'd like to stop that too.

Even if just because my interfering would make her so very, very angry."

She bit off the thread and put the needle back in its protective sleeve. She looked approvingly over her handiwork, but it just looked like a bunch of black bundles to Scout.

Daisy looked up at her again. "So I need you to promise to step up. The next time you have a gun in your hands and a dire need to take out someone who is going to murder you the moment they're done murdering me and probably make you watch them kill your dogs first, take the shot."

Scout nodded, not trusting herself to speak. The last bite of crackers and peanut butter coated her mouth like sticky dust.

"Good enough," Daisy said, her tone suddenly bright, and Scout realized she was talking about the little bundles in her hands.

"What are they?" Scout asked.

"For the dogs, silly," Daisy said, sliding one over two of her fingers to demonstrate. "The palms of the mittens are this denser material with kind of a knubby texture to aid in gripping. Perfect for booties with grippy soles. These are going to work just great. Now, why don't you get some sleep? I don't really need sleep myself, not more than a few minutes. Plus, I have a spare scarf in my pack that should be big enough for two dog-sized balaclavas."

Scout curled up around the dogs, burying her nose in Shadow's soft fur and warming her hands under Gert's snout.

She had thought this would all be over once they got inside the city. But that was just going to be the beginning.

And she had no clue where it was all going to end.

15

WHEN SCOUT WOKE, the tent was almost uncomfortably warm. The dogs had moved away from her to sprawl their legs out. She had taken her coat off at some point.

The little glowing heater wasn't even on anymore.

Daisy was already awake. Or, perhaps more likely, she had never slept. When she saw Scout's eyes were open, she immediately set a mug of something steaming within arm's reach.

"I was about to wake you to get going," Daisy said as Scout sat up and sipped at the beverage. She had no idea what beverage it was trying to be, only that it wasn't quite pulling it off.

"Yeah, I know," Daisy said, seeing her face. "The water up here boils too soon to make a proper cup of tea. But it's hot and has an extra shot of caffeine, so drink it up anyway. The storm stopped a few minutes ago."

Scout wondered how she could tell, as silent as it had been inside the tent all night long. She tried not to grimace as she drank the tea. She could feel the caffeine stirring up inside her, so much less unpleasant than the stim had been.

Daisy opened a container of some sort of meat in a rich sauce, and the dogs were awake in a snap, rushing to fill their bellies. When they finished, they sat back to lick the gravy from their lips and quite willingly allowed Daisy to fasten the booties to their paws.

Scout found a protein bar in the side pocket of her pack and munched on that while she straightened her own clothing, rebraided her hair, then reached for her coat.

That was odd. She could have sworn it had been distinctly heavier the night before. How far up the mountain had they come?

"I took some plates out of it," Daisy said when she saw the look on Scout's face. "It will make you lighter."

"Why?" Scout asked.

"The snow has blown up in some interesting arrangements," Daisy said. "We might need to test a few places that look like they're on a trail but aren't. I'm too heavy, and I can't make myself any lighter."

"So I'm going to be walking in the front?" Scout asked.

"Yes, Scout," Daisy said with a wry smile, "I'm asking you to scout."

"I don't think I can push up a trail as you did," Scout said.

"You won't need to for you or the dogs," Daisy said. "About an hour ago, we had a brief blast of sleet; then the temperature dropped very low. The snow has a nice crust on it now. You'll be able to walk on top of it now that I've reduced your weight. Plus, I've consolidated the packs to just what we need, so you won't need to carry one."

Scout looked around and saw that indeed Daisy had an oversized pack beside her, and the one Scout had been carrying was mostly empty, sitting like a deflated bladder beside it.

"Did you sleep at all?" Scout asked, feeling guilty for how deeply she had been slumbering while Daisy did all this work.

"I require very little," Daisy said. "But I promise you I got what I need. I'm not irresponsible."

"No, I wouldn't think so," Scout said.

"Finish that protein bar," Daisy said. "You're going to need the energy, and it's too cold out there to unwrap your face if you get hungry later."

"It's going to be a long day," Scout sighed.

"I'm afraid so," Daisy said. "And we can't dawdle in getting it started."

Scout stuffed the last of the crunchy, fruity, honey-sweet bar in her mouth, then started layering her goggles, hat, and scarf over her head.

Daisy was fitting little balaclavas over the dogs' heads. She had sewn in goggles to fit over their eyes and a more breathable fabric over the noses of the balaclavas so that the dogs, too, would have their faces completely covered. With the vests and the booties, they should stay perfectly warm this trip.

Daisy left her pack on the floor as she headed out the opening in the tent, pushing snow away ahead of her as she cleared the tunnel she had dug the night before that the storm had almost completely refilled.

Scout looked at the empty pack. That might come in useful later. She folded it tightly and stuffed it inside Daisy's pack.

Then she saw the gun lying on the canvas floor of the tent. It had been underneath the pack, and Scout wondered if Daisy had forgotten it was there.

It was more likely to come in handy than the empty pack, but still, she was loath to touch it.

Without letting herself give it a second thought, she snatched up the gun and tucked it in the loop at the back of her marshal's belt, where Gertrude Bauer's gun had gone before Scout had lost it.

That little bit of extra weight just felt right. But that rightness made Scout almost sad. What sort of life was she choosing for herself? Or being driven to choose?

Weak sunlight suddenly filled the tent and Scout knew that Daisy had broken out. She grabbed the pack and dragged it behind her as she climbed up through the snow to the world above, the dogs scrabbling up after her.

It was intensely bright in the morning light. There was very little exposed rock left, just a world plastered with fresh snow that reflected every bit of light from every possible angle. Scout was grateful for the tinted goggles.

The dogs beside her were confused by the booties on their feet. It was like they didn't know how to put their paws down or weren't sure through the fabric if they were actually touching the ground or not. Shadow clambered about with paws spread wide like a four-legged spider, a staccato dance that seemed to deeply startle him.

Gert, as usual, minded the change less.

But neither of them were slipping on the slickly frozen snow. Daisy had been right about the gripping soles.

"Let's get up there first," Daisy said, pointing up. Scout's eyes took a moment to pick out the rocky promontory that jutted high into the air. The snow sticking to all of its sides made it blend with the distant strands of white cloud behind it.

"What about the tent?" Scout asked.

"We can't spare the time to dig it out," Daisy said. "I have the other from your pack. I doubt it will snow so hard again."

"I hope not," Scout said, but she couldn't argue about the time it would take to dig the tent out. It had been buried under nearly two meters of snow. No wonder it had gotten so warm on the inside.

The dogs saw Daisy climbing the rock and raced to follow her. Shadow danced over the frozen top of the snow, but like Daisy, Gert was too heavy and kept busting through. The poor dog found this very frustrating, as it slowed her down considerably.

Scout followed Daisy up to the highest point on the rock. The mountain itself was behind her, the dome atop it gleaming even more brightly than the snow. The mountainside spread out before them, all uniformly white now.

"There's the village," Daisy said, pointing as if she knew Scout couldn't make out any details. "The cabin, and the other cabin."

"I see them," Scout said, although she wasn't sure she did. The dots were so tiny. Had they climbed so far already?

"And there are our pursuers," Daisy said, pointing again.

There were three separate groups of dots, not much bigger than the dots that made up the village, only these dots were moving. One group was following a ridge, walking in single file. Another was scaling a rock face with the jerking start and stop motions of climbing. The third was following the trail they had taken the night before. Scout guessed they had just passed the flat place where the three assassins had tried to ambush them.

"There might be others we can't see," Scout said. "They might be closer."

"Maybe," Daisy said. "But I wouldn't worry. None of these are making any effort not to be seen. They know we know where they are. They just don't care. They're that confident."

Scout remembered how they had just disappeared before blowing up the tram station. Whatever camouflage they had used then, they weren't using it now. "So what do we do?" she asked.

"Get to the city before they get to us," Daisy said, like it was the simplest thing in the world. Then she turned to face the mountain, scanning everything in front of her before pointing off to her right. "There."

Scout had to shade her eyes from the gleaming of the city's dome to see what Daisy was pointing at, and even then she wasn't sure if she was seeing anything at all.

"A trail?" she ventured.

"It will be clearer when we get closer," Daisy said. "Just go back down the promontory and start following the ridge off to our right. The dogs will follow you, and I'll bring up the rear."

"Okay," Scout said nervously. She wasn't sure she was up for this responsibility, but she couldn't work up the courage to say so out loud.

It was weird. That feeling of not wanting to disappoint Daisy was growing even stronger than her fear that Daisy would find out what Scout had done to her sister. But she needed Daisy to get to the city; she would never be able to do it alone.

Scout walked carefully over the top of the snow. It squeaked beneath the soles of her boots, and although the top was all little whorls and ridges like dunes of sand, it didn't give under her weight, not even enough to leave a boot mark where she had gone.

Occasionally, something far below her would shift. The icy crust didn't break, but she could feel just how much snow was between her and solid rock, and just how treacherous it could be. If the crust she was walking over cracked, all that snow was waiting to swallow her up. Swallow her up and carry her like a river far down the mountain, under the icy crust, into a deep, cold darkness she would never escape...

Scout gave herself a little shake and forced her mind to stop imagining worst-case scenarios. If she did fall into a hole in the snow, she'd likely just be pinned up to her knees until Daisy pulled her out. Daisy and the dogs were only a few paces behind her. Nothing irreversible could happen in less time than it would take for Daisy to get to her. She would be fine.

The sun climbed higher into the sky, finding a less glaring angle off of all the snow, if not exactly warming the air. Scout looked back at her dogs trotting happily behind her and was immensely grateful for the sleep Daisy had given up in favor of fabricating little outfits for the dogs.

At some point in the future, long after Shi Jian was no longer a threat to the galaxy and the fate of Amatheon had been decided in the tribunal court, when she had a moment for such things, Scout was going to have to find a way to properly thank Daisy.

Somehow; she had no idea what Daisy liked, what gesture would be meaningful to her.

The ridge ended in another plain of snow, and Scout drew to a halt. She could see the snow on her right ending in a feathery edge and remembered what she had seen when looking around from the promontory. She suspected this was one of the curlicues of snow blown off a ridge to curl downward in a frozen wave.

"Why are you stopping?" Daisy asked as she and the dogs reached Scout.

"I'm not sure how much of this is rock and how much is snow with a long drop below it," Scout said. Daisy scanned the plain, moving her head in tiny deliberate adjustments from left to right.

"Stay closer to the left," she advised. "Even if it is just snow, it's very thick here and frozen on top and bottom. It should be strong enough to hold your weight."

"But what about your weight?" Scout asked.

Behind her goggles, Daisy was giving her a dry smile. "Just stay closer to the left. We'll both be fine."

Scout nodded and turned back to face the plain. She took a deep breath, and then she took a step.

Then another. And another. It felt just as solid beneath her as it had before. Which wasn't entirely heartening—the image of a river of snow waiting to swallow her up still lurked in the back of her mind—but it was the best she was going to get.

Scout risked a glance up from her own feet and saw the plain ending in what looked like the snowy outline of a human-made bridge. The sides were so straight and so parallel, and its body rose at such an even, gentle arc to the center before falling away again. Surely snow didn't just blow itself into such an even shape?

And behind the bridge was something very like a road, one side hugging the side of the mountain, the other a sheer cliff, but its edge was clearly defined by stone markers that stood starkly up out of the snow. Walking up that path was going to be a joy.

Scout stepped out onto the bridge. The cold snow still squeaked under her feet, but there was no deeper creak or rumble, no feeling of deep beds of snow shifting beneath her. She continued on over the arch of the bridge and down the other side to the waiting road.

The snow wasn't so deep here, close to the mountain. This must have been the leeward side of the mountain last night when the winds were blowing the snow around. It had been spared.

Scout grinned at the feel of solid rock under her feet, then turned to put her hands on her knees as the dogs came charging down to her.

This had to be a road that led all the way to the city. Why else would there even be a road here?

Daisy's head appeared over the apex of the bridge, and Scout gave her a friendly wave, not sure if she was even looking up enough to see her.

Then her shoulders were visible, then her swinging arms, and she must have seen Scout waving at her then, as she raised a hand in salute.

And then she was gone, without so much as a crash of snow or a yelp of surprise.

She was just gone.

16

THE DOGS both started barking like crazy, and Scout bent to grab their collars in case they were about to charge back up the bridge to help Daisy.

Scout didn't think it likely that Daisy had just fallen down, but she held on to that hope for several long minutes. Maybe she really had just fallen, despite how vertical her descent had appeared to Scout. Maybe she was about to pop back up, dust herself off, and join them on the other side.

She held on to that hope for far longer than she should have, but she didn't really grasp that fact until the first dart whistled past her ear.

Then the dogs were barking again, a deeper warning. Scout threw her arms up over her head and looked around, but her perfect road built for easy walking provided no cover whatsoever. She would have to make a run for it, hope she didn't get hit before she could make it around the curve of the mountain…

She was never going to be that lucky. Another dart whistled past her and Scout felt a rush of anger. They were aiming not to hit her; she was suddenly sure. Like they were having some sort of game of who could come the closest.

Scout unzipped her coat and pulled the gun from the holster on the back of the marshal's belt. She didn't give herself time to think. She could feel the indecision and guilt and waffling about to wash over her in a tidal wave, and she knew she didn't have even a second to act before she would be in over her head in all those emotions.

She fired.

She had aimed in the general direction of the assassins flocking to the edge of the snowy plain on the other side of the bridge, but she hadn't drawn a bead on any one of them in particular.

To her surprise, they flinched back, crouching and retreating at her wayward shot. Had they expected her just to stand there and wait to get hit?

Scout ordered the dogs to back away from the edge, then shuffled closer to it herself, trying to see the bottom of the ravine.

Again, it took her eyes a long time to turn the field of bright white into features with definition.

Then she saw it: a flash of motion. Directly below the bridge were tall mounds of snow that must have shifted off of structures above, pouring down to get hung up here where the ravine was at its narrowest. And protruding from one of the mounds of snow was a pair of waving arms.

Daisy. She was fighting to pull herself out, but the snow kept shifting beneath her heavy weight. Scout's hand twitched, about to wave down to her, but she held it back.

The assassins on the other side might not know she was down there, or they might think she had died or been grievously injured in the fall. Daisy was going to need a minute to get herself out. Scout would have to be sure she got that minute.

The assassins were creeping up to the edge of the ravine again. Scout saw two of them aiming long-barreled dart guns at her. She was sure they weren't aiming to miss this time.

Scout held the gun in both hands and pointed it at the larger target of the two assassins with guns. She squeezed the trigger, then watched in horror as the bullet bounced off a rock nowhere near the assassin.

She could swear through the dark mask she could see that assassin grinning at her as they aimed their weapon.

Then there was a low rumble, and Scout stumbled back from the edge, not certain where the sound was coming from. It echoed all around her, and she was terrified it was coming from above her, that she was about to be buried under tons of smothering snow.

Then she saw the bridge shiver. Cracks shot across the surface, branching like lightning bolts. A few chunks broke away to tumble down in agonizing slow motion.

Somewhere in the back of her brain, Scout knew this slowness was because of the low gravity, but it still felt like the universe was doing it for dramatic effect, to mock her.

Then the entire bridge sheered away from the cliff and plunged down to land in the deep snowy mounds below, throwing up a cloud of swirling flakes that spun all the way up to where Scout stood, obscuring her vision of the assassins on the far side.

And vice versa. Scout turned and ran, the dogs close at her heels, not stopping until she was around the curve of the mountain, out of range of the assassins' weapons.

Without the weights in her coat, she was considerably lighter. Not as light as she had been on Amatheon's moon—that had been true microgravity—but light enough to run in long, ground-eating bounds that made her faster even than her still-weighted dogs. It would almost be fun if she weren't constantly feeling like darts were already zooming towards her exposed back.

When she was certain she had reached a safe distance, she skidded to a stop, collapsing to the ground with a dog on either side of her. Her nanite was working properly, but she was still getting winded quickly.

That bridge had fallen directly on top of Daisy. Daisy, who had still been trapped in the mound of snow.

Shi Jian, with her body modifications, had once survived a trip through the vacuum of space with no apparent harm. Were Daisy's modifications as advanced? Were they enough to keep her alive in the smothering, cold dark beneath all that snow?

Scout bit her lip and thrust her head back against the cliff wall behind her in frustration.

She was going to have to go back. She had to get to Daisy, somehow.

She had to get down into the ravine and across all of that loose snow, snow she had no idea of the true depth of.

And she had to do it without being seen.

Scout hugged both her dogs tight, then took out their leashes and fastened them to an outcropping of rock.

"Sorry, guys," she said. "I have to get Daisy or we're all dead, but I can't try taking you with me. I don't even know how I'm going to get down there, let alone you. But I'll be back."

She pulled down her layers of scarf to give them each a kiss, then bundled back up her scarf and coat both. She put the gun in her coat pocket where it would be closer to hand if she needed it again.

You know, in case she wanted to trigger another massive avalanche.

Scout pressed herself as flat to the ground as she could, then crawled to the edge of the road. She could see the assassins gathered at the far edge. Had any of them fallen down the ravine? Scout quickly counted heads. No, they were all there.

One small favor. She didn't want to have to fight any augmented assassins lurking at the bottom of the ravine on top of the dangerous climb down and the still-uncertain task of digging Daisy out.

One thing at a time.

She had to get to the bottom of the ravine. Quickly. But she had no climbing equipment. She might have had some yesterday, but now everything was in Daisy's bag.

Down there, at the bottom of the ravine.

Scout bit her lip again to stop the vicious cycle of her thoughts. The assassins on the other side were working together, assembling a larger sort of gun. Scout frowned in confusion; what were they aiming at?

Then she saw two of them fire bolts to secure the gun's tripod into the ground, and another of them holding a long coil of rope.

They were coming across to her. She had to act, now.

Scout fought the urge to laugh maniacally out loud. There was really only one way down, and there was no point in dawdling, hoping for another solution.

Scout looked down to the bottom of the ravine one more time.

It was deepest in the center. And hopefully—she bit back a wave of rabid fear on how little concrete data that hope was based on—*hope-*

fully less likely to be hiding a rocky protrusion there, farthest from the walls.

Scout got up and took a few steps back, ignoring the excitement of the dogs, who thought she was coming back to them.

If she died doing this, they would die too, tied to a wall until they starved or killed by the assassins out of spite…

No, they would be just as dead if she stayed with them, without Daisy and all the equipment. She had to do this.

Scout took a deep breath and ran forward, bounding along the road until she reached a steeper part of the curve.

Then she launched herself up and out as hard as she could.

For a moment, she felt like she would keep flying up forever. But then her momentum slowed. She reached a hand out as if she could catch hold of one of the clouds above her, or the glimmering flash that might be a ship coming down to dock.

Then she started to fall.

She wished she had thought this through more. Should she pull her arms and legs in tightly, like a torpedo? Or would that just bury her too deep to climb out again?

Would she smash like a rotten tomato if she flung her arms and legs out wide to spread out the impact over as much snow as possible?

She hit bottom before she even had time to decide. Her heels touched down first but slipped out from under her, and she landed on her buttocks.

Then she was flat on her back, but by that point, she was already sliding over the frozen crust of the snow. She was picking up speed, but even when she managed to lift her head enough to look down at her feet, there was nothing to be seen past the spray of snow she was throwing up into the air.

If any of the assassins were looking down now, they'd surely see her.

Had she screamed when she jumped? She didn't think she had, but her mind was already repressing the memory of that moment.

She reached the low point between two snow mounds and slipped up to the top of the next one without appreciably slowing down. She tried dragging her mittened hands to slow herself down, but the crust was too thick to punch through, and she could get no purchase.

Then her feet collided with the remains of the bridge, and she stopped with jarring suddenness.

Scout sat up and looked around. Where had Daisy been?

Then she looked up and was relieved to see none of the assassins looking back down at her. But they would have that gun rigged soon enough, and she had to get back up onto the road to retrieve the dogs before they did.

Scout climbed over the remains of the bridge. She was sure Daisy had been just a little further downhill.

Then she saw a skitter of snow, a layer of debris from the bridge dancing over the still-frozen crust of the snow mound beneath it. She looked back up the slope until she saw another skitter form, small bits of snow hopping up into the air then sliding down, catching at others.

She scrambled over to it and started punching through the ice.

Daisy would have to hear that, at least.

She kept at it, breaking open the crust with her fist, then crawling a little further along to punch again. If Daisy could swim through the snow, she would find the last bit easier to get through.

She hoped the shattering of the crust wasn't as loud above as it was below, echoing along the narrow walls of the ravine.

A rush of snow slid behind where she sat on one hip, punching ice. It buried her feet and legs up to her knees, and she turned over onto her back to scramble away.

Then the snow looked like it was boiling up like an angry anthill, wave after wave of ants spilling up and out, only this was all snow.

Then it erupted, snow exploding everywhere. Scout wiped wet chunks off her goggles and saw Daisy on her hands and knees, breathing in deep gulps of the thin mountain air.

"Thanks," she said, her voice a hoarse croak.

"The pack?" Scout asked.

Daisy was still breathing hard, but she turned a bit so Scout could see the pack still on her back.

That was a relief.

"We have to get back up to the dogs," Scout said. "The assassins are getting ready to fire a line across. We don't have any time."

Daisy nodded and pushed herself to her feet. Scout ran ahead to lead the way back to where she had jumped. By the time she reached the indent in the snow where she had landed, Daisy had regained her breath.

"Climb on my back," Daisy said.

"Are you sure?" Scout asked. Daisy didn't look even half recovered from her time under the snow.

Daisy didn't speak, just nodded. She turned to face the wall, finding handholds and footholds before Scout had even worked out a way to get up on Daisy's back. She hopped up, wrapping her legs around Daisy's waist. It was awkward, draping over the bulky bag, trying to interlock her feet in the heavy boots, and Daisy grunted as she took Scout's weight.

But then she started to climb, an insanely fast crawl up the cliff side, hand and foot, hand and foot. Scout resisted the urge to hang on more tightly, aware that her arms were already cutting off Daisy's breathing. Instead, she just squeezed her eyes shut and waited for the herky-jerky journey to end.

She gave a little yelp when Daisy was suddenly sprawled out horizontally under her, but she opened her eyes and realized they were once more on the road. Scout climbed off Daisy and crawled forward to quiet her anxious dogs before they could start barking.

Then there was a loud retort, echoing all around them.

The gun with the rope. They had fired it.

Loose bits of snow were dislodging from the mountain over them, raining down in powdery clumps. One the size of a snowball landed on Shadow's head and he groaned in protest.

Daisy picked her head up and looked at the three of them.

"We've got to move," she said and forced herself to her feet.

Scout didn't need to be told twice.

17

IT WAS easy to make fast time on the road, Scout bounding as high as she dared, the dogs sprinting alongside her. Daisy looked like she was maintaining an easy jog, but she was keeping pace with them without any trouble, and Scout knew if she put on the steam and left them behind, Daisy would probably be in the city by lunchtime.

The road curved ahead, following a deep groove in the mountainside. Scout followed the path of it ahead of them with her eyes as the groove went from valley to deep but narrow ravine. The path followed the ravine until it ended as if at a wall, a space no wider than Scout could spread her arms.

Then the path turned and came back the way it had come, back up the ravine but on the far side.

Scout could see a point where she thought she could simply jump across, saving quite a bit of time by not following the road along the entire curve.

But that left a long expanse to run down first, meters where the chasm that was too wide to jump, but the road would be well within weapons' range. A very long expanse, and it was completely exposed.

"They're too close behind us for this," Scout said over her shoulder.

"No other way to go," Daisy said. "Look, there's a cave or tunnel or whatever on the other side. We just have to get to it. We'll have cover there."

"We'll be easy targets up to that point," Scout said.

"So will they."

Scout didn't find that comforting. There were six of them. Three for Scout and three for Daisy.

Even if it was one for Scout and five for Daisy, Scout still felt greatly outmatched.

The dogs kept charging all the way to the end of the switchback, but Scout jumped across at the first place she was confident she could reach the other side.

The dogs would catch up. And they were unlikely to be targets. They were only in danger so much as Scout was in danger. She had to get to cover for their sakes as much as her own.

"Heads up!" Daisy shouted just as Scout landed on the far side of the ravine, stumbling forward into the cliff wall and bumping her nose hard enough to bring a metallic taste to the back of her throat. It must be bleeding, but she wasn't going to unwind the scarf enough to check.

Daisy had stopped in the middle of the road, firing her gun until their pursuers ducked back behind the cover of a rocky protuberance. Scout drew her own gun and fired, not aiming at anyone in particular, just driving them further back around the corner.

They would be back, but at least Daisy had enough time to get across now.

The dogs ran past Scout, tongues lolling as they panted, but they seemed to know what the end goal was. Scout put her gun away, and despite not having caught her breath, she pushed away from the ground, forcing her legs back into the bounding rhythm.

Just a bit further. She could see the tunnel. It was so distant it appeared tiny, but she could see it.

Daisy gave another shout, but it wasn't enough warning this time. The air around Scout was suddenly full of darts. How could six people fire so many at once? They were like swarms of angry wasps hissing through the air, bouncing off the rock wall behind her.

Scout put her head down and tried to run harder. Even in the heavy boots, her ankles wanted to turn; her soles threatened to slip over icy patches disguising themselves as rocks.

Her muscles were burning. She was getting tired. Not enough recovery time between these bouts of athletic prowess.

Another vision invaded her mind: herself, tumbling all the way back down the mountain after falling off the edge of the road. The world turning end over end with jumbled views of the village growing ever larger as she picked up speed, tumbling towards it.

That was silly. Surely she'd hit her head first, and everything after that would just be black nothingness.

Scout heard the loud cracks of Daisy firing her pistol once more, but the cascade of darts plunking all around Scout didn't slow. More bits of snow were sliding down from above, raining down on the road around Scout. Gert dodged around a particularly large clump, her wide paws stumbling frighteningly close to the edge of the road before she lurched back to the cliffward side.

Then she and Shadow disappeared into the darkness of the tunnel. Safe.

Scout's legs were on fire, her muscles starting to twitch in random quirks that didn't help her bounding at all. Even with the nanite, she couldn't seem to get enough air. Black nothingness started to eat at the edges of her vision, closing down to a pinpoint that was just the mouth of the tunnel in front of her.

Scout had pushed herself this hard on her bike before. She hadn't quit then when nothing was on the line but her own pride and, to be honest, boredom.

There was no way she was going to quit now when it actually mattered.

Daisy yelled a fearsome cry and sent another volley of gunfire across the ravine. This time, the darts did stop. Scout thought she heard Daisy give a shout of triumph, but it was hard to tell, her heart was beating in her ears so loudly.

Then she reached the darkness of the tunnel, a welcome change from the blinding snow. Scout shoved the tinted goggles back onto her forehead, but as she collapsed against the side of the cave, she saw the effect wasn't complete. The edges of her vision were still dark. Were her glasses broken?

She turned her head, looking back out the tunnel mouth to Daisy sprinting toward them, and realized it wasn't the glasses. It was her eyes.

Or more likely something in her head. At any rate, the black closing in around her didn't mean her glasses were broken.

It meant she was passing out.

Wow—she had no idea she had gotten so out of shape.

Scout bent forward, hands on her knees, and waited for the feeling to pass, but that just made the slipping-away feeling intensify.

The dogs were looking up at her, heads tilted in questioning concern. She tried to give them a smile, but with all the layers of scarf around her face, there was no way they could see it.

Scout's muscles were still doing that random firing thing. They were also tightening up, like everything in her body was trying to make a fist at once, fists so tight they ached.

Then the ache kicked up to outright pain, and Scout groaned as she fell to her hands and knees. The dogs rushed forward to lick at her, or at least lick at her clothing. Scout tried to brush them back, but her hands had become fluttering, useless things.

She managed to sit back on her heels and tried to massage away the pain in the back of her neck. She jerked her hand away as something sharp pricked at her finger.

Then she reached back again, to see what that prick had been.

Daisy reached the tunnel mouth just as Scout figured out that it was a dart there on the palm of her mittened hand. She held it up for Daisy to see.

Then she pitched forward. She was vaguely aware of a fresh burst of pain as her still-sore nose collided with the stone floor of the cavern.

But not even the pain could hold her in the world. Which was just as well; she felt another spasm of muscle seizures gripping her just as her mind slipped away to blissful black.

18

IT HURT TO BREATHE. Scout would draw air in until the knives stabbing between all her ribs made it impossible to inhale further. When she exhaled, it was like her lungs were pulling away from the sides of her chest cavity as they deflated, tearing something all around her insides.

Then she'd breathe in again.

She couldn't draw a full breath; the knives made that impossible. She almost wished she could just stop; the pain was so unrelenting.

But she had a vague sort of memory that she had stopped breathing at some point a moment before her awareness had returned, and that had been an entirely different kind of horror. So she kept moving the tiny amounts of air through and tried to figure out what was happening to her.

It felt like something was sitting on top of her chest, pinning her down. Or maybe her whole body; her arms and legs felt cold and remote. Had there been another avalanche?

No, there had been a dart. She remembered that part clearly.

Scout struggled to open her eyes. It hurt, like her eyelids had become adhered to her eyeballs and were tearing away bits of flesh as she lifted them. But she couldn't whimper or cry.

Not with those knives digging into her chest.

At last she got her eyes part of the way open, the most she could manage physically but more than she needed given the blinding whiteness of the world outside.

She had forgotten about that, the brightness of it. She blinked a few times, not as fast or as hard as she was trying to, but enough to be sure her eyes were really focusing.

Her glasses and goggles were gone. No protection against the sunlight reflecting off the snow.

She was just about to close her eyes again, to shut that brightness out, when a shadow eclipsed the light and she realized she wasn't out in the snow. She was in the tunnel, several meters away from the mouth.

"Scout," Daisy said, and Scout realized it was Daisy's body blocking the light. "Just rest easy. I gave you the antidote, but I was nearly too late. The dart was loaded with a paralytic. Reversible, and every assassin carries the antidote. It was in both of our packs. Which tells me Shi Jian really does want to take you alive."

She leaned closer, and Scout felt Daisy's warm, bare hands on her cheeks as she gently lifted Scout's eyelids and looked into her eyes.

"Which leaves one question," Daisy went on as she continued her examination. "These assassins fired on you when you were too far away for them to reach you in time, especially as they knew I was there and prepared to stop them getting to you. And unless they did a post-battle inventory, which isn't protocol, they didn't know I have the antidote. Risky. So, did they mess up on accident or on purpose?"

Scout heard Gert make a soft whine, then her field of vision jostled back and forth. Gert was leaning up against her? She couldn't feel it at all.

"Don't worry, girly-girl," Daisy said to Gert. "She'll be okay in a few hours."

Scout heard another groaning noise but realized this time it was coming from the back of her own throat. A few hours was nearly all the daylight they had left.

The other assassins had to be closing in on them even as they sat here hiding in a tunnel that was the most obvious hiding place, being directly on the only road Scout had seen.

Daisy moved out of Scout's field of vision. Scout heard rustling sounds, like Daisy was digging through her pack again. Then there was the skitter of dogs' nails on the stone floor as the two of them left Scout's sides to rush to where Daisy was setting something down on the floor.

She must have heated it up, whatever it was. Scout could smell roasted meat and carrots.

Her stomach growled. That must be a good sign, right? That her stomach wasn't paralyzed?

Daisy came back to where Scout could see her, still smiling a smile that Scout knew was meant to reassure her.

Scout gathered all of her energy and just managed to croak, "Go."

Daisy frowned. "No," she said.

Scout narrowed her eyes, drawing her brows down sternly. She had practiced a lot of nonverbal communication during her time with the tribunal enforcers. Daisy clearly understood that Scout was trying to repeat her command for Daisy to go on without her.

"No," Daisy said again, more firmly. "Not even. I already told you, I came to get you because I need you. I'm not going on without you, so you can stop glowering at me like that. No."

Scout gave up with a sigh. At least the knives were easing now. She could breathe something closer to normally.

"Why?" Scout managed to whisper.

Daisy moved out of sight, then returned a moment later with a steaming mug in her hands. She sat down on the tunnel floor, turned sideways so she could see both Scout and the world through the mouth of the tunnel beyond the feasting dogs. She glanced both ways as she took a first tentative sip from her mug.

She grimaced. "Low air pressure is a bitch," she said, but drank her tea, anyway. "I'm not sure which '*why*' you mean, but I'll give it a shot because I need you to stay awake and keep breathing. The antidote works faster if you're awake and trying to do things rather than lying inert. Understood?"

Scout couldn't nod, but her head lolled in a way that Daisy took to be agreement.

"Why won't I leave you behind? I just told you," Daisy said, counting off one finger. "Why did I come here to get you? Ditto." She counted off another. "Why do I need your help? Well, you're connected to galactic marshals, that's handy. You know who Shi Jian is and what she's capable of. I'm sure you can see how difficult it could be to try to convince a stranger of the danger she represents. You couldn't even convince Bo Tajaki, and frankly, he should've known already."

Scout made a grunt of protest, and Daisy scoffed before taking another swallow of tea.

"Whatever—he should have. Anyway, I don't have a lot of choices for allies. I watched you while you were on his ship, and I know I can trust you."

"How?" Scout asked. Speaking was coming a bit easier now, but the rest of her body was still cold and heavy.

"How?" Daisy repeated. "That's more complicated. Short version: I was hiding in the walls of the ship. I've been invisible to the ship's systems for… quite some time. I saw you arrive and researched everything they had on you in the Tajaki trade dynasty databases. Then I hacked Shi Jian's private system and read up on her take on you. Shi Jian rotates her passwords regularly and keeps her security systems tip-top and up to date, but I can always get past those because I watch when she does stuff. She suspects someone is getting past her, but she's never figured out who or how."

Daisy smiled smugly into her tea, then took another drink.

Then her smile slipped away as if it had been painted on a mask that had just dropped off her face.

"I came from the surface of Amatheon too, you know," she said. "My sister and I. Our parents died during the war. Like yours. Well, not from one of the rock strikes. There was more close-up fighting inside the capital. One day, my sister and I came home from school, and our parents just weren't there. It was a week before anyone told us they were dead. Collateral damage when Space Farer and Planet Dweller forces got into a brief exchange of gunfire near a marketplace."

She looked away from Scout, out through the tunnel mouth to the wintry landscape beyond. Nothing was moving out there except a few low-hanging clouds.

"We didn't have anyone else to take care of us. We were sent to an orphanage that was all kinds of terrible. They split us up. I guess lots of folks think my sister stopped talking when our parents died, but that wasn't it. It was after that first night she had to sleep in the dormitory with the other girls her age, away from me. I don't know what happened. Maybe nothing happened except that I wasn't there. I don't know. She never spoke to me again, not so much as a nod or shake of her head to confirm or deny my worst fears. She was just... gone. Everything that had been my sister, gone, leaving this shell behind that still looked like her."

Scout was glad it was too much work to try talking. She didn't want to even try to find words of comfort about Clementine. Clementine had freaked Scout out from the very moment they had met, Scout and her dogs both.

"Anyway," Daisy said, turning back to look at her tea. "Shi Jian found me first. I had escaped the yard. I wasn't running away, just wanted an afternoon a little less regimented for a change. She caught me stealing sweets off a cart, and at first I thought she was with security. She wasn't wearing a uniform, but you know how she is. She just feels like authority.

"But she wasn't. She bought me a whole paper cone of sweet fried pastry dough and a huge cup of lemonade. I had never had lemonade before. Or that pastry thing; I don't even know what it was called. Fritters, maybe. Well, you know. Rich kid stuff, right?"

Scout managed something like a nod. She had never had lemonade herself.

"Then she told me I didn't have to go back to the orphanage, that she had a better place for kids like me, where I would get to learn how to do the most amazing things. And that I would be able to make everyone who ever hurt me pay."

Daisy looked down at her tea, turning the mug around and around in her hands.

"I'm ashamed now, how much that appealed to me then. But I told her no. I couldn't go anywhere without my sister.

"And she said, 'Wonderful! Let's go get your sister.'

"And she just signed us out all official-like, and the next thing I knew I was back with my sister, eating more sweet fried dough and riding a shuttle up into orbit like it was the most normal thing in the world."

Daisy drank the last of her tea in one long swallow.

"Well, you saw the school. Not extensively, but enough, am I right? You saw what she does to kids. Not all of it, but you got the sense."

She kept glancing over at Scout as if checking that Scout was indeed agreeing with each of her assumptions.

"I didn't take to it," Daisy said, her mouth twisting as if the last dregs of her tea had been particularly bitter. "But Shi Jian 'believed in me,'" she said, making air quotes with fingers capable of taking an opponent out with a jab to the right nerve bundle. "She wouldn't let me go. I went through all the physical modifications, and all the mental modifications were tried on me. Even though I wouldn't conform, she wouldn't let me go.

"There had been others who didn't conform, of course. All sent out on missions they never returned from. I suspected they had been suicide missions. Not that those kids had known or even suspected. I mean, who among us really knows what they put inside us when they were swapping out our bones and blood and organs? Could be anything, right? I could have a kill switch inside me right now and not know it."

Daisy stepped out of view again, returning with a fresh mug of tea and settling back in the same spot on the tunnel floor. The dogs came up to her, sniffing around in case she had brought more food as well. Daisy reached out a hand to scratch Gert around her ears and rub at her neck, but she didn't even seem to be aware she was doing it.

"I suspected. I prepared. And when my name was up, I disappeared. But I didn't leave. I couldn't leave. My sister was still there. I stayed inside that ship, hiding where no one could find me. And they never did.

"But she still managed to take my sister away."

Scout's nose was itching. She reached up a hand to scratch it but overshot, striking her nose hard enough to make herself wince.

"Hey, you're moving!" Daisy said with a smile. "Arms, then legs, then we're back on the road and none too soon. See, dogs, I told you she'd be okay."

"Daisy," Scout said. It was irritating how just the act of talking was exhausting her, but she pressed on. "Are we after Shi Jian to stop her from doing something bad, or for revenge?"

Daisy sat back, the smile once more gone from her face.

"I plan to kill her," Daisy said. "It serves both ends. What difference does it make, which one is the real reason why?"

Scout gave a short nod, but her stomach was forming a hard knot, and not just because she was hungry.

Daisy wanted to kill Shi Jian because she blamed her for Clementine's death. What would she do if she found out that however much Shi Jian had been to blame for what Clementine had become, it was Scout herself who had dealt the killing blow?

Would she even let Scout try to explain?

Scout closed her eyes and let her head fall back against the stone wall behind her.

Better she never knew. Which was easy enough to say, but in Scout's experience, secrets never stayed secrets. It was just a matter of time before Daisy found out.

Which was better, to know sooner or later? Would the two of them growing more and more reliant on each other make her feel more bonded to Scout, or more betrayed?

Scout really, really wished she knew.

                                     19

SCOUT WOKE from a doze when the entire world around her started to shiver, a low rumble building to a roar all around her.

Avalanche. They were going to be sealed up in this tunnel like a tomb, with just enough air to starve to death or freeze to death over the course of many days and nights.

Scout saw skitters of snow dancing over the road outside the tunnel, a few larger balls of snow shattering into powder on impact, but nothing large enough to do even the dogs any injury.

"Run!" Scout cried and scrambled to her feet.

Or at least she tried to. She had seen newborn animals on farms back home make a better show of it.

Daisy caught on to her, holding her up on her feet but not letting her run out of the tunnel.

"We have to get out of here!" Scout said.

"No," Daisy said, then to the dogs, "stay!"

The dogs needed no such direction. They were huddled together, far from the tendrils of snow blowing in from where the balls had impacted. They wanted no part of what was going on outside.

"I don't want to be buried alive," Scout said.

"Of course not," Daisy said. "If it blocks the tunnel, I'll dig a way out, but for now, we're safer here."

Scout could see the sense of that. She stopped trying to get past Daisy and just watched as the skitters of snow slowed to a halt and the rumble moved on down the mountain, only the faintest of echoes remaining to dance through the tunnel.

"You're doing better," Daisy said.

"It's nearly dark," Scout said, trying not to sound as disappointed as she felt. She had fallen asleep. If she had stayed awake, they might have moved on by now.

Why had Daisy let her fall asleep?

"We can't bed down here," Daisy said. "It's bad enough they haven't jumped us yet. They probably know they hit you and not me. I'm not sure what plan they'll make around that information. If it were me, I would have attacked already."

Scout didn't doubt that.

Daisy quickly repacked her bag and slung it on her back, then came back to Scout to make sure her cold-weather gear was all on correctly: glasses and goggles and hat secure, coat zipped up, boots fastened snugly.

She felt like Daisy was treating her like a surrogate little sister, but she couldn't summon up the energy to object. Maybe Daisy needed to feel like a big sister. Scout could tolerate it, at least until the lingering effects of the dart weren't making her feel like half a toddler herself.

Daisy kept hold of Scout's arm as she led her down to the other end of the tunnel. Scout kept her eyes focused straight ahead, waiting for the dot of light that would grow into the mouth of the far end of the tunnel.

But the light never came. They reached the end of the tunnel to find it nothing but a wash of snow, with not even the narrowest beam of light anywhere.

"This just happened?" Scout asked miserably. Why had she napped so long?

"Maybe not," Daisy said, but she didn't sound convinced.

"What do we do now?" Scout asked.

"Hold on," Daisy said. She tried climbing up onto the snow, but it wouldn't hold her weight. At last, she just accepted that fact and charged forward, pushing snow ahead of her until she had blasted a narrow path past the drift of snow and back out onto the open road beyond.

"See?" she said as she came back for Scout.

"It sounded bigger than that," Scout said.

"Sound is weird in tunnels," Daisy said. "And around mountains. That last one might have been nowhere near us."

Scout was about to agree when they walked around a curve in the mountain and the road once more disappeared under a drift of snow.

But this drift went on for as far as Scout could see.

"Can we walk across the top of it?" Scout wondered, but Daisy didn't even have to answer. Perhaps it was the sound of Scout's voice, perhaps it was some other stimulus, but little pebbles of snow started sliding down the drift, building up speed and number until an entire sheet of snow was moving, sliding off the end of the road to fall to the bottom of the ravine.

The ravine was deeper here. A lot deeper.

"Maybe we don't want to risk it," Daisy said, and Scout flinched at the way she didn't even try to lower her voice.

"Can you really plow it all the way across?" Scout whispered. Daisy was up on tiptoe, shading her eyes against the setting sun as she searched for any sign of the road on the far side.

Scout realized with a start that they must have circled half the mountain for the setting sun to be visible. She turned to look up at the city and was promptly blinded by the dome reflecting the rosy light.

"Up," Daisy said at last, and Scout looked over to see her also looking up, but not at the city. "The road has another switchback ahead of us, then continues back in this direction. It's right above us."

Scout put out a hand to cover the shining city and looked at the rock face towering over them.

"Are you sure?" Scout asked. She saw no sign of any road or any switchback at all.

"Very sure," Daisy said.

"It doesn't matter," Scout said, giving up trying to see it. "I can't climb that wall. The dogs certainly can't."

"That's true," Daisy said.

"You can climb the wall."

"But I can't carry you all," Daisy said.

"No, that's not what I meant," Scout said, although that made for quite the image. "You should climb up on your own, get to the city."

"I'm not going after Shi Jian alone," Daisy said, wearily reviving that argument.

"No, but you can come back for me with more help," Scout said.

"If I leave you here alone, they'll be on you in a hot second," Daisy said.

"Fine," Scout said, crossing her arms. "What's our other option?"

Daisy looked around, tapping her mittened fingertips against the scarf over her face. Then she looked around again.

Gert sat down on the road for a brief moment, then went all in and sprawled out to take a nap.

"Well?" Scout said.

"I'm climbing up there," Daisy said.

"Good," Scout said.

"But I'm coming back for you," Daisy said. "I have rope. I'll go up and find something sturdy to tie it to; then I'm coming back down for you and the dogs. However many trips it takes."

"You'll be target practice for all of them if they see you climbing," Scout said.

"I'll be fast," Daisy promised.

"I believe you will be when you're on your own, but what about when you're bringing the rest of us up?"

Daisy sighed. "Scout, it's the only plan."

Scout drew her gun, and Daisy gave her a sharp nod. Then Daisy was scurrying up the cliff side, her hands and feet finding holds Scout couldn't even see.

Scout looked around for any signs of ambush. Nothing was moving on the road on the far side of the washout of snow. Not that Scout thought they could have gotten around her and Daisy, anyway. The far side of the ravine was a jagged ridge, with no spots wide enough for anyone to stand on. An assassin trying to fire from there would need to scale the ridge to get up there and would have to keep holding on with one hand while firing, and they would be completely exposed. Not to mention the only place they could have come from was the ravine below, now filled with snow.

No, Scout was certain the only avenue of attack was the tunnel they had just emerged from. She turned to face it, gun in her hand but not yet raised.

She glanced up at Daisy. It took a moment to find her, far above Scout and the dogs on the road. Then her feet kicked out as her top half disappeared, and Scout realized she had reached the road above them.

A moment later, a rope came snaking down, then Daisy appeared over the edge again, using the rope to rappel down the cliff to land with a heavy thump in front of Scout.

"Did you take a look around from up there?" Scout asked. "Any signs of the assassins?"

"Yes, I did, and no, there isn't," Daisy said, reaching around Scout's middle to tie some sort of belt around her waist. "This attaches to the rope. It will catch you if you slip. I'll come up behind you with the dogs."

"Both of them?" Scout said.

"I can take the weight," Daisy said. "I left the pack up there."

"They might squirm around, especially if they're together," Scout said. "Let me take Shadow. He barely weighs a thing."

Daisy considered this for a long moment, then conceded with a nod, helping Scout make a sling out of the outermost of her shirts to hold Shadow close to her chest, zipped up inside her coat, leaving her hands free to climb.

Scout stepped up to the rope and gave it a little tug as Daisy fastened the belt to the rope and tested the catching device.

"Ready?" Daisy said, clapping her on her shoulder.

Scout nodded, hoping that nod looked more assured than she felt. She had never climbed a rope before.

She gripped it in her hands and looked up at the long expanse of rock waiting for her.

"Put a foot here," Daisy said, showing her a small outcropping that was somewhat flattish on top. "Then your other foot there. Hold the rope like it's a railing, like this is just a very steep ramp."

"Maybe you should go first," Scout said.

"No," Daisy said, shaking open the empty pack Scout had stuffed in the top of Daisy's pack. She had found it and brought it back down with her. Daisy didn't say a thing about it, but Scout was very grateful for the impulse to keep it. Daisy hugged Gert, then stuffed her in the pack before the big black dog had a chance to object. "I have to go behind."

"You said this catch wouldn't let me fall," Scout said.

"It won't," Daisy said. But if that was true, there was no reason for her to be under Scout, was there?

Scout didn't think arguing about it was going to accomplish anything other than burning time, and it was already getting dark far too fast. She had to be on the road above before the sun disappeared or she'd never finish the climb.

Scout used the holds Daisy had shown her. It felt weird leaning back with the rope in her hands, and she was all too aware of the road behind her back. She felt a rush of dizziness and forced herself to take a deep breath.

If she fell here, hitting the ground would be a jolt. But if she got dizzy again further up?

She had to keep her head clear, her mind focused.

She opened her eyes, saw another knob of rock that could function as a foothold, and took the step, pulling herself up the rope even as she found the next step for her other foot.

"Good," Daisy said. "Just like that. You're doing great."

Scout felt Shadow squirming against her stomach, but Daisy had tied him in too tightly for him to move more than that squirm. He was just flexing his muscles and whining. Scout tuned him out and took the next step.

She was not even a third of the way up before her arms started to ache.

The ache was an agony by the halfway point. Scout tried to take more of her weight on her toes, but even that little adjustment had her body waving back and forth on the rope. Her feet nearly slipped from the little outcroppings she was using as footholds.

"You're doing fine, Scout," Daisy said. Scout didn't dare look down, but it sounded like Daisy was moving even more slowly than Scout, her voice drifting up from a point barely off the surface of the road. "Keep going. You know, I found some chocolate in the food rations. We can split it when we get to the top."

Scout forced the whiny part of her mind to acknowledge that standing still was just as exhausting as climbing had been, and it fell silent long enough for her to press on.

Sunsets on Amatheon had always been lazy affairs, the large red orb that was its sun sinking slowly behind the western hills, the orangey light of dusk a welcome relief after the intense heat of midday. She could stop her bike the first moment the sun kissed the horizon and set up camp, cook some food, and share it with the dogs and still be able to watch the last of the sun disappear while sprawled out on her bedroll.

Sunset on Schneeheim, on the other hand, was more like a person switching off a light. One moment Scout could see the next few footholds in front of her, the next she lost sight of them all together in the sudden darkness.

"Daisy?" Scout called.

"You're nearly there," Daisy said, still far behind her. "Just a little further."

Scout turned on her night vision. It took a moment for her eyes to work out where those holds were. Looking at the green-tinted world wasn't the same as the world in full daylight, but she could adjust.

Scout could see the stone markers that stood at the edge of the road above her. She was nearly there. Her arms were shaking, her hands trembling so violently it took time to force them to close around the rope after moving them, but she was nearly there.

Just a few more steps.

Then Daisy gave a yell of alarm, and Scout heard the soft thunks of darts striking the rock face all around her.

20

SCOUT DUCKED HER HEAD, for all the good that would do her, but it was a reflex. The darts were coming from directly below her. The assassins must have come through the tunnel like she had feared.

And Daisy, with Gert on her back, was taking the brunt of it.

But she couldn't look down. She had to get to the top.

Scout let out a yell of equal parts rage at their pursuers and pain from her exhausted body. She charged up the last few footholds and then really had to work her arms, reeling herself in until she could pull herself over the ledge.

The dog tucked close to her stomach made that more complicated than it would have been otherwise, and she had to twist sideways to drag herself up on one hip before rolling over onto her back, staring up at the dark gray sky above her, hugging Shadow close with two shaking arms.

She wanted to just lie there forever, to sleep for a million years and never move again.

But that wasn't an option.

She sat up and forced her trembling hands to unzip her coat and untie the sling to let Shadow go. He scrambled away to sit against the cliff on the far side of the road. It would be a while before he forgave her for what had just happened.

Scout rolled over onto her belly and slid up to the edge of the road, looking down at Daisy and Gert, barely at the halfway point of the rope.

The assassins were no longer firing darts, and Scout didn't see them on the road below—but that was only because they were climbing the rope behind Daisy, scaling the cliff with the fast pace Daisy had managed when she was climbing alone.

They were closing in on her fast.

Scout pulled out her gun and took aim, but with all the assassins lined up behind Daisy, she couldn't get a shot.

Daisy looked up and saw what Scout was doing. She paused in her climbing to look around, and Scout wanted to scream in frustration. She needed to move faster, not slower.

Gert's head was looking up over Daisy's shoulder. Either Daisy had packed her that way, or she had squirmed her head out of the opening on top. Scout really hoped it was the former.

Despite everything going on around her, Gert looked absolutely thrilled, tongue lolling. Then Scout saw that Shadow had come to stand beside her, looking down at his doggy friend.

"Scout!" Daisy called up to her as she detached herself from the rope and swung her body onto a parallel track. "Take the shot!"

Scout raised the gun. She was about to gently squeeze the trigger when a sudden fear gripped her.

It was like she could feel all the snow still on the mountain behind her, looming over them all.

What if the sound of her gun firing triggered another avalanche? Was that possible?

"Scout!" Daisy growled up at her. She was making her way up without the rope, but at any moment, the assassins would see what she was doing and abandon the rope as well.

"Hello, Teacher," Scout said through gritted teeth.

"Hello, Scout," Warrior said, appearing beside her, also lying on her belly and looking down the cliff. "Take the shot."

"What if I trigger another avalanche?" Scout asked.

Warrior looked around. "Unlikely. Everything that was going to slide already did so."

"Are you sure?" Scout asked desperately.

"Scout!" Daisy shouted, loud enough for the assassins to look up and see Scout there aiming a gun down at them.

"If you don't take this shot, possible avalanches won't matter," Warrior told her.

Scout saw one of the assassins moving away from the rope, taking a diagonal path to catch up with Daisy and Gert.

"The only shot I can take is a headshot," Scout said. "But that would kill even them, I think."

"They aren't giving you a choice, Scout," Warrior said.

Scout bit her lip. She couldn't let the assassins reach Daisy and Gert. She definitely couldn't let them get up to her and Shadow. Scout was sure Daisy could fight off any attacker even while scaling a cliff, but Scout would have stood little chance even before she exhausted herself climbing.

She couldn't let them get up here, but did that mean she had to murder them? Was that really her only choice?

She was haunted by what Daisy had said almost in passing about the mental conditioning that hadn't taken hold of her own mind. All of these kids had been susceptible to it, but was that unfixable now? Could they be redeemed if given a chance?

Could they just be kids again?

"Scout!" Daisy cried again, this time ending in a frustrated shriek as her pursuer caught hold of one of her ankles. She kicked their hand away, then followed that up with a kick to the face that snapped their head back sharply and nearly knocked them off the mountain.

Nearly, but not quite. And after clinging where they were for a moment, they continued their pursuit.

And the others on the rope had nearly reached Scout and Shadow.

Scout aimed the gun for the rope. As shaky as her hands were, she didn't think she could hit any of the assassins until they were right on top of her, but if she severed the rope…

She was aiming for the point on the rope directly in front of her gun barrel, and it still took three shots to hit it. But when she hit it, it blasted apart at once, the weight of the climbers snapping it back with the speed of a retractable cord.

Scout heard shouts of alarm and felt snow pelting her shoulders but ignored both, focusing instead on the climber once more reaching for Daisy's foot. Scout fired, again and again, wishing she had taken out her slingshot instead. Aiming the gun wasn't remotely the same experience. Firing her slingshot was instinctive to her. She never even thought about aiming. She just did it, aim and fire all in one smooth motion.

She had no such instinct with the gun. But the fifth or sixth shot struck a protruding rock just in front of the climber, spraying their masked face with sharp slivers of shattered stone. They threw up a hand to protect their eyes—foolishly, as the mask protected them; it must be one of the younger kids—but Daisy had been watching for just such an opportunity and let herself drop back far enough to kick at their other hand. They slipped, caught a different hold, then slipped again, falling with a scream that ended abruptly the moment their body hit the road.

"They can survive that," Warrior told her. "But recovery will take time."

Scout turned her attention back to the path directly below her. Two of the assassins had let go of the rope and were still climbing up to her. When Scout fired again, she swore they both just let go of the rock face, letting themselves plunge back down to the road.

"What was that all about?" Scout asked.

"Regrouping," Warrior said. "They're going to be coming after you again."

One of Daisy's hands appeared over the edge, then the other. She clutched a stone marker and pulled herself up to collapse facedown on the road.

Scout turned to tell Warrior to go, but the AI had already disappeared. Not the first time she had seemed to read Scout's mind. Perhaps they shared the feeling that Daisy didn't need to know all of Scout's secrets.

Although Scout kind of suspected Daisy knew all about Warrior, anyway. If she had been hiding in the walls watching everything, she probably had seen Bo gift it to her in the first place.

"Give me a minute," Daisy said, wheezing into the ground. Scout found the tie for the pack on her back and opened it enough to let Gert fall out of it.

"Are you ill?" Scout asked, sitting next to Daisy's head.

"No," Daisy said, then forced herself up onto her elbows. "I require a specific form of sustenance, and I've run out. I can maintain with normal food, but I would need a lot of it. Even if I ate everything we have and left nothing for you and the dogs, it wouldn't be enough."

"The same is true of them," Scout said, looking over the edge. None of the assassins below them were stirring yet.

"Yes," Daisy said.

"But you stole their packs."

"They only had a day's supply on them."

"So these guys might be getting hungry," Scout said. "That will slow down their recovery time, right?"

"It would, but I suspect they are getting resupplied," Daisy said.

"How?" Scout asked.

"Those vehicles we saw outside the cabin, maybe," Daisy said. "They might have found the other end of this road. It would have taken them some time, but eventually, they would have met up with the groups that followed our trail over the rougher terrain."

"Should we get off the road, then?" Scout asked.

"No, we're nearly there," Daisy said, sitting up. "And off-road here means more cliff climbing. I don't know about you, but I don't think I can do it again. Not without rest and proper food."

"No, the road is better," Scout said, but she didn't like it. Everyone knew where they were. There was no way to hide.

They would have to move quickly. And she was already so very tired.

"I wonder if we could trigger another avalanche," Daisy said, tipping her head back to look at the top of the cliff high above them. Even with Scout's night vision, it was hard to distinguish where it ended and the sky began.

"No," Scout said. "If my gun didn't set it off, I don't think anything will."

"I have explosives," Daisy said, patting the pack she had left leaning against the cliff wall.

"No," Scout said again. "We're as likely to bury ourselves as them, and we really don't have the time."

"Onward, then," Daisy said, getting to her feet and bending to pick up her pack. She huffed out a breath as she pulled it up onto her shoulders.

"Do you need me to carry that for a while?" Scout asked.

"No, I've got it," Daisy said. "Maybe you can take point?"

"Of course," Scout said.

It was strange talking to someone when you were both wearing goggles with layers of scarf around the rest of your face. The smallest tilt of a head suddenly carried tons of meaning.

Scout was pretty sure that Daisy had just given her the tired but hopeful smile she herself had been trying to give Daisy. Scout was glad she was there. There was no way she would have come so far without her. They would have gotten her for sure that first attack on the plateau in front of the McGillicuddys' cabin.

Scout looked up at the mountain as they walked. She could no longer see the dome of the city, not because the sun was no longer gleaming off of it, but because they were now walking almost directly beneath it. Not much longer and they would be there.

And then the real fight would begin.

21

THEY WALKED HALF the night before Scout could not take another step. Daisy didn't look like she could do much more either and found them a niche in the cliff a short climb up from the road, far enough that once they were inside no one walking by would notice them.

It was a tight squeeze, but that was probably all for the better, as the temperature started dropping again. Daisy pulled a thin, insulated blanket out of her pack and huddled close to Scout with the dogs between them so she could tuck it around all of their bodies.

Shadow curled up in Scout's arms, his preferred place to sleep. Gert usually liked to be behind Scout's knees, but now she had another human at her disposal. She curled up against Daisy, resting her head on Daisy's biceps and closing her eyes with a very contented sigh.

Daisy had her goggles pushed back and her scarf pulled down around her throat. Scout could see her face as she looked down at the dog sleeping against her. Her expression didn't change much from its usual hard, stoic look, but there was a definite warm fondness to her eyes as she put a gloved hand on Gert's big head to caress her softly as she slept.

Scout felt another sharp pang in her heart for all the secrets she was keeping. Daisy felt like a decent person who would take circumstances into account, and if it were just what Scout had done, she would confess it.

But Gert had attacked Clementine, too. And it was for Gert's sake that Scout had stabbed Clementine in the one place she couldn't recover from.

If Daisy knew, would that fondness leave her eyes? Even that would hurt Gert. There were a lot of things short of murderous rage that Scout still desperately wished to avoid.

She liked Daisy. There was a comfortable feeling between them that reminded her of her childhood days with her family and school friends. She didn't want to lose that.

But what could she do to prevent it? She could only keep her secret for so long, and she was sure once they were in the city, she would have to confess. The moment they weren't running for their lives.

She owed Daisy that much.

Scout felt like she had only just shut her eyes when Daisy was sitting up, gathering up the blanket to stuff it back in her pack.

There was no sign of the sun, although the gray of the world around them wasn't dark enough for it to still be night.

"Another storm?" Scout asked, looking around at the clouds scuttling darkly all around the mountaintop. It was disorienting how many of them were blowing by below them.

"Or the same storm back again for another pass," Daisy said. She took out a protein bar and snapped it in half for the dogs, then gave another to Scout.

"What about you?" Scout asked, her mouth stuffed with the sticky berry crumbs.

"I ate already," Daisy said. "I'll be fine. Just think, once we're in the city, we can find some proper tea."

Scout nodded. She wasn't much of a tea drinker herself, but she could see the naked longing for the beverage in Daisy's eyes. Scout preferred the fizzy, caffeine- and sugar-laden jolo, but as it was always served ice cold, she had no craving for one now. But back on the prairie after a hot day pedaling a bicycle? Nothing better.

The rising sun competed with the darkening clouds, leaving the world around them a consistent murky gray. Great flakes of snow were dancing through the air, not falling exactly, just riding the faintest currents of wind.

Scout reckoned it was about midday when the road curved around one last protrusion of rock before finally reaching the city wall. She recognized the stonework: stacked blocks that seemed older than time, just like inside the station where she had gotten on the tram.

The road now circled the city itself in both directions, curving out of sight without any sign of a door or gateway.

"Which way?" Scout asked.

Daisy looked both ways, then stood still for a long moment with her eyes unfocused.

"I'm not sure," she said at last. "I don't have any record of an exterior door from my time inside the city, but there must be one somewhere, or else why the road?"

"Is the road as old as the wall?" Scout wondered, touching the carefully smoothed blocks. "When they put up the dome, they might have blocked all the exits except for the trams."

"We'll find something," Daisy said. "But for now, one way is as good as the other. To the left?"

Scout shrugged, and they started walking in that direction.

The wall was more than twenty meters tall, not as far as they had climbed before, but Scout could see that Daisy was beyond exhausted. Putting one foot in front of the other was the most she seemed capable of.

Scout wasn't eager to try climbing again anyway, especially not without a rope. Each of the blocks was as tall as she was; she would have to grasp handholds with her fingertips and somehow pull herself up...

Scout shook her head. It would be impossible. And there was nothing above them but the bottom of the dome, resting without the slightest gap on top of the wall.

The wall had no windows, no doors, no openings of any kind.

The snow was falling thickly when they reached a part of the wall that housed a tram station. It jutted out over the road without supports.

"I wish we could see the doors from here," Scout said, but even leaning as far as she dared from the furthest curve of the road showed only the side of the boxy station facing her. It was made of similar stone to the city wall itself, and whatever was holding the far end up must have been built into the floor itself. Nothing else was visible.

"It's closed anyway," Daisy said wearily. "The storm."

Scout couldn't argue with that; the snow was coming down just as densely as it had when they had shut down the trams before.

Still, maybe there was a way to open it from the outside.

"Maybe we should climb up there just to see?" Scout said hopefully.

"If nothing else presents itself, we'll come back," Daisy promised, sounding even more tired than before.

Scout looked at the way the end of the station jutted far beyond the edge of the road. If she should try climbing out there and fall...

Scout leaned out over the edge again. Yep, it was a long way down.

"Okay," Scout agreed.

The setting sun and the growing storm were making everything so dark Scout had to turn her night vision back on.

Daisy kept her own eyes on her feet, as if she needed to concentrate all her energy on keeping them moving.

Scout was worried that they would have to stop and camp again—she had so been looking forward to being inside the warm city with a belly full of warm food—when the dogs started barking.

They weren't on the road. It took Scout a moment to realize that the edge of the road was no longer a steep drop-off. Now there were a few meters of steep rock fall before the drop-off, and the dogs were down in it. They were both barking down the same hole.

Scout wondered what sort of animal could survive in this environment, completely exposed with nothing like a food source for kilometers.

Then she noticed the way the dogs' barks were echoing. How deep was that hole?

Scout carefully picked her way down to the dogs. The larger rocks tipped under her feet, and the smaller ones slid against each other, readily creating mini avalanches with every step she took. She was more than half convinced she would fall off the mountain before she reached her dogs.

Having safely plummeted down to the bottom of the ravine wasn't making her feel any better about her odds of surviving an accidental fall.

Shadow was gone from sight by the time she reached the mouth of the hole, but Gert was waiting for her, the white tip of her tail a blurred arc as she wagged her entire back end in excitement.

Then Shadow poked his head back out of the hole to look up at her, his fur glowing ghostly in the darkness. Scout fished around in her pockets until she found a light, then bent down to shine it into the space behind Shadow.

It wasn't an animal warren at all. It wasn't a naturally forming cave either; not with those perfectly rounded walls.

Then she directed the light further in and saw the dull gleam of metal.

"Daisy!" Scout called. "The dogs found a way in! I think I see a door down here."

She pulled her head out of the tunnel and straightened up, but Daisy was already picking a way down to her. She moved just as carefully as Scout had.

"What kind of door?" she asked. They both poked their heads in, and Scout directed the light to the end of the tunnel.

"I think it's an old one," Scout said. "We should climb in, get a better look at it."

They had to get down on hands and knees to accomplish it, and they had to crawl in single file—except for Shadow, who managed to squeeze past both of them to be the first one to the door. He sniffed at the green and orange patches but didn't seem to like what he smelled.

"Rust?" Scout said, not wanting to touch it.

"Some kind of algae or lichen, I think," Daisy said. "It's warmer here. Shine the light around the edges. Let's see if there's a lock or handle or something."

They carefully examined every centimeter of the metallic hatch, but there was no sign of a way in.

"Fine," Daisy said, lying down on her back. "I'll try kicking it down."

"Are you sure you're up for this?" Scout asked, but Daisy didn't answer.

The sound of her boots impacting on the metal over and over was like some kind of industrial machine: loud, precisely timed.

And never ending. After dozens of blows, Daisy quit, flopping back to look up at Scout.

"No good," she said. She looked even grayer than before, and Scout knew she had just burned far too much of her energy reserves.

"You said you had explosives?" Scout said.

"Yes!" Daisy said. "I forgot about those. Stupid brain fog. Yes, help me get this pack off."

A few minutes later, Scout sat on the road a couple of meters past the tunnel opening, holding a dog tightly in each arm. Then Daisy appeared outside the hole, bounding up to the road in three great jumps that made Scout want to scream with fright. If just one of those steps came down on the wrong rock…

But Daisy landed next to her just as a muffled thump shook the ground beneath them, sending a cascade of rocks off the edge of the cliff.

"Should be clear now," Daisy said, making her way more carefully over the loose rock back to the opening. Scout let Gert go, and then Shadow once Gert was safely inside the tunnel.

Then she picked her own way down, stooped so low she was nearly crawling. She had thought the last trip down had been hairy, but it was worse now that they had shaken everything loose. She slid more than once, catching herself each time, but by the time Daisy's hand closed on her wrist and pulled her into the tunnel mouth, her heart was hammering like mad.

"Let's not do this again," Scout said. "I've had enough of mountains, I think."

"Agreed," Daisy said. "But we did it." She pointed, and Scout shone her light down the tunnel. The metal hatch had burst in three segments, curving in like the petals of a flower to open the way inside the wall itself.

"Shall we?" Daisy asked.

"You don't want to take a nap or something first?" Scout asked, only half joking.

"We can nap when we're back among friends," Daisy said. "I can make it another hour if you can."

"Yes, let's nap in actual beds," Scout agreed.

"I'd settle for a couch," Daisy said as she led the way through the blasted hatch, making her way gingerly over the jagged metal. It only looked as soft as a flower.

"I can make do with the corner of a room if it's warm," Scout said, making sure both dogs were ahead of her before crawling through the hatch.

The air felt warmer already, and so full of oxygen it flooded her brain like pure energy.

She was supercharged. She could handle anything.

Shi Jian had better be watching her back.

22

THE TUNNEL SPIRALED UP, and Scout knew they were heading in the right direction to come up under the city, but it was a slow, lazy spiral that seemed to go on forever. Even through the thickly padded clothing, Scout's knees were growing sore from all the crawling.

The dogs kept racing on ahead, out of sight. Scout would call them back, but each time they returned with greater reluctance.

"Any idea where this comes out?" Scout asked.

"I'm actually worried that it doesn't," Daisy said. "I have more explosives, but I don't think we could get to a safe distance in time in these conditions."

Scout hadn't even considered that, that their nice spiraling tunnel could end in another sealed hatch.

Or maybe no hatch at all. They might be walled off, an old section no longer needed when the new city was built on top of the old.

No, she told herself. The air and warmth were coming from somewhere. And the dogs were racing forward into the darkness again with an eagerness that could only mean they smelled something they desperately wanted to get closer to.

Scout sniffed the air. She sneezed from the dust their crawling was stirring up, and the chief smell was an old musty odor, like she imagined a newly unsealed tomb would have.

But under that, just faintly, she smelled… roasted potatoes?

"I see light!" Daisy said and started crawling faster. Scout couldn't see around her well enough to make out anything but the walls her shoulders were brushing against, but they seemed a brighter shade of gray.

Then she heard the dogs whining, jumping up and down in excitement. Daisy drew to a stop and sat down, and Scout saw the dogs were standing at the bottom of a hole in the low ceiling, light shining down on them like they were the stars of a show.

She could hear sounds: a murmur of voices, the low rumble of a vehicle, all very far away.

"How do we get up there?" Scout asked.

"I can climb that and lower a rope," Daisy said. She slipped the straps of the pack off her shoulders, then quickly found the other thin strand of rope and looped it around her neck. Then she stood up into the hole, bracing her back against one side and her feet opposite, and just shimmied up the pipe-like space.

Daisy's body blocked out all the light, but Scout could hear her little grunts of breath as she climbed. Those stopped and there was another sound, a rustle of clothing while Daisy dug out a tool, and then a soft scraping sound.

Then there was a louder clang as she threw back the grate and light once more shined down on Scout and the dogs.

Daisy waved from the top of the pipe, then dropped one end of the rope down to Scout. Scout tied it around both dogs' vests and gave it a sharp tug. Daisy reeled in the dogs, who yelped in surprise, then squirmed in excitement as they realized they were getting closer to the smells.

Scout cursed herself for not sending the leashes up with Daisy. How far would the dogs run off while Daisy was busy bringing Scout up out of the hole?

The dogs' bodies blocked out the light again, and Scout listened to the sounds of Daisy hauling them up out of the hole, then untying the rope.

Then nothing. Scout looked up into the light but saw no sign of Daisy or her dogs. She couldn't hear anything either, just the background murmur from before.

Just when she was starting to really panic, the rope dropped out of nowhere, plunking her on the head. Scout put on the pack and grabbed the rope. Daisy was hauling her up, but Scout was all too aware of how run down Daisy was and took all of her own weight she could by mimicking Daisy's climb up the hole.

Then she was out in the yellowish light, throwing her weight forward as she grasped with her hands. Daisy grabbed a fistful of the back of her pants and hauled her out of the hole, then gently replaced the grate.

Scout looked up to see both dogs looking at her, tails wagging. Then they dropped their heads again, licking intently at the tattered remains of some sort of cardboard food basket.

"You found that?" Scout said.

Daisy looked over at the cardboard. "Yeah. We're near the marketplace. Someone missed the trash and left most of their fried potatoes behind as well. But the dogs sure enjoyed it."

"Shame the dogs didn't leave any to share," Scout said, her stomach growling. The smell of roasted—or perhaps fried?—potatoes was stronger here.

Now that she was sure her dogs were safe, Scout took a proper look around to see just where "here" was. It appeared to be an alley between two of the tall towers, lit by slightly off-putting harsh yellow lights. The alley was paved with cobblestones that felt slightly sticky, and other bits of trash had drifted against the walls.

It wasn't an alley people walked down much, Scout guessed. Neither tower looked to have any doors, and the far end of the alley ended at the city wall.

But the other end offered the narrowest glimpse of a street with more pleasant lighting and the occasional pedestrian or two, most carrying bags filled with their purchases. It felt like the middle of the night to Scout, but she guessed it was still early evening by the number of people carrying what looked like covered plates of hot food with them.

It must be that holiday Mary Grace had told her about, the one with the feasting.

"Come on," Daisy said, putting out a hand to help Scout to her feet. "There's an information station at the marketplace. Who are we going to try to get to first?"

"The McGillicuddys," Scout said.

"We can get directions to their place there," Daisy said. Scout fished the leashes out of her belt pouch and clipped them to the still-distracted dogs. "We should get rid of our coats first."

Scout took off the pack and then her coat. She had taken off her hat, goggles, and scarf in the tunnel and stuffed them in the pockets. Daisy pulled out the empty sack she had used to carry Gert, put both their coats inside, and handed it back to Scout.

"Won't we look odd, walking around with packs?" Scout asked.

"Not in this town," Daisy said. "Lots of tourists coming and going from the port; we'll blend right in. But wearing coats inside the city would be odd."

Scout took up both of the leashes, and they walked out to the street. It wasn't hard to guess which direction the marketplace lay. Aside from being where the package-laden pedestrians were coming from and the food-laden ones were walking to, as well as the growing murmur of voices, the smell of potatoes and roasted meat was like a lure guiding Scout along.

"You know the city well?" Scout asked, watching Daisy tick off cross streets on her fingers one by one as she murmured the names.

"Not really. But I took complete schematics from the city database. Nothing with people's names attached, or I could save us this trip, but I can find the chief landmarks besides all the streets."

"Just how long were you here before I got here?" Scout asked. "The Torreses said people had been asking about me. Was it the assassin kids? How did you all get here so fast?"

Daisy raised a hand at the barrage of questions. "Slow down, one at a time. First, yes, I arrived with the rest of Shi Jian's kids. I was watching them from my hiding place in the walls. Bo was watching them on cameras, which they spoofed, but I was watching them with my own eyes through a grill. I saw them take out the guards and then go out an airlock, and I blended in with them. I still had my uniform, and the procedure called for full masking, so that worked in my favor."

"Full masking?" Scout asked.

"Just what it sounds like," Daisy said. "Perhaps you thought you couldn't see anybody's face because it was cold? I guess that would be part of it, but Shi Jian sends us on two kinds of missions: missions where we masquerade as kids and infiltrate a place openly, and missions where we're meant to be invisible. Full masking is for the latter."

"I guess you didn't have any missions of the former kind that involved all of you at once," Scout said.

"No, not until this one," Daisy agreed. "So I went out the airlock with the others, and I don't know how Shi Jian did it, but she had an entire shuttle docked there, invisible to any of the ship's systems. Not like a tribunal enforcer ship, where it's invisible to the eye but apparent to ship systems; more like the opposite. We all got in, and the shuttle took us to another ship, but we never left the shuttle. Not for the entire trip through hyperspace."

"Still," Scout said. "I left first. How did you beat me here? I thought tribunal enforcer ships were state-of-the-art or whatever?"

"That's what I've been trying to tell you," Daisy said. "Whoever Shi Jian really works for, they are leagues beyond the tribunal enforcers or even the Tajaki trade dynasty with their tech. Shi Jian's body modifications are beyond any of ours or the galactic marshals, and the Tajaki trade dynasty didn't give her any of that. I don't think even Bo knows half of what she can do. And this ship was another example of it. We made the trip through hyperspace so fast we beat you by a full day."

"I don't like the sound of this," Scout said. "This keeps happening. I know I'm already in over my head, and yet it always turns out there's another level above me and I'm even deeper than I thought."

"I know," Daisy said. "We just need to focus on one step at a time, and the first step is right here."

She pointed to what looked like a larger version of Emma McGillicuddy's desk nook, or rather a series of them, all along the low wall that contained the marketplace. One or two had people standing in front of them, asking for directions or leaning close to consult the map displayed on the angled surface. Daisy stepped up to an open unit but typed in her request rather than speak it out loud.

"I'm getting the directions for the Torreses as well. Just in case," Daisy said.

"You can remember all that?" Scout asked. Daisy gave her a look like she wasn't sure if Scout was joking. "You have augments for that too?"

"Too many things," Daisy said. "But at the moment, they're coming in handy, so I won't complain too much. The McGillicuddys' apartment isn't far from here. We should go around the marketplace rather than through it, though. Better maybe not to be seen."

"Sure," Scout agreed, but her stomach growled in protest at being dragged away from those marvelous smells.

Emma would have food. And Scout was sure that her tea would be up to even Daisy's exacting expectations. Scout hadn't paid attention at the time, but she was curious now how Emma got around the low-boiling-point-at-high-altitude problem.

Daisy led them around the marketplace wall and then down a smaller side street, away from the center of the city and towards the city wall. Then she ducked down an even smaller street before stopping at one of an endless row of exactly identical doors.

"This is it?" Scout asked. She could see no markings of any kind.

"This is it," Daisy said and skipped up the three shallow steps to push the button.

Nothing happened. Daisy pushed it again, holding it a moment longer.

After the third try, Scout fished out the door-opening device she had on her marshal's belt. Daisy stepped back as Scout set the little box over the part of the door containing the locking mechanism. The little light on the side of the box went from red to green, and the lock clicked open, the door swinging ajar.

Beyond the door was a long corridor filled with still more doors, all closed, all unmarked. Daisy led the way to the correct door, then pushed the call button and rapped on the door itself loudly.

Her augmented knuckles made an impressive boom. Scout could

hear it echoing through the apartment beyond, as well as up and down the hallway.

But still, no one answered.

"Maybe they're out," Scout said.

"Maybe you should open this door, too, so we can be sure."

Scout set the device on the door again. The light turned green, and the door was open.

They didn't bother to step inside. The entire apartment was visible from the doorway, and it was completely empty.

"You're sure this is the place?" Scout asked.

"Yes. Unless they moved without updating the city directory, but there are fines for that."

"No luggage, no food in the kitchenette over there. I don't think they ever got here," Scout said.

"No, no one has been here for days," Daisy said. Scout didn't ask how she knew that. Given the way she seemed to be smelling the air, Scout really didn't want to know.

"They might have gone straight to the Torreses," Scout said. "Because I stayed behind, or because they felt like it would be safer together, maybe."

Daisy swept her eyes over the room one last time, then stepped back and shut the door.

"I hope you're right," Daisy said and led the way back out of the building.

Scout wasn't sure she was right. She had a tight feeling in her stomach, a growing certainty that everything had gone very bad up here just as it had down in the village.

And from the tightness of Daisy's jaw, Scout guessed that Daisy felt the same.

23

THE TORRESES' apartment was on the far side of the city. Daisy led the way, first towards the marketplace, then up to the top of a five-story building to catch the next transport. The roof was open to the air and Scout could see the dome curving down to meet the wall only a couple of blocks away. They were at the very edge of the city.

There was a small crowd waiting when the train arrived, but not so many that they couldn't get one of the small cars to themselves.

Scout settled onto the seat, and the two dogs hopped up to sit on either side of her. This station was on top of the building, not in the heart of it, and Scout could see the city through the windows even before the train started moving. They followed a level rail that ran parallel to the city wall, curving around the outer edge of the city, skimming over the low buildings.

The gentle swaying of the car as it glided along the rail was hypnotic, but the train stopped at too many stations for Scout to drift off for more than a moment or two. The little not-quite-naps were leaving her feeling more exhausted than ever, and she could feel the beginnings of a headache tightening up behind her eyes.

"When are we going to get food for you?" Scout asked after being lurched back awake yet again.

"When we get to Shi Jian," Daisy said. She was starting to look distinctly gray.

"Maybe we should stop so you can eat however much normal food you need to make up some of the difference?" Scout suggested.

"No," Daisy said. "Thanks for looking out for me, but I'll be okay. I just want to see this through. And it's probably irrational, given that most of her assassin army has to be still out there in the snow, but I've got this nagging feeling like time is running out."

"I'm feeling that too," Scout said. "I kind of doubt we're both being irrational."

"Me too," Daisy sighed.

The car was suddenly plunged into darkness and Scout start to rise to her feet up in panic, but then she realized they were just pulling into a station that was inside a taller building. She had been looking at Daisy and hadn't seen it coming.

"This is us," Daisy said, turning towards the door as the car braked to a standstill. Scout gathered up the leashes and followed Daisy out onto a nearly empty platform. One man was just stepping into a car on the other end of the train, and a sole woman was sitting forlornly in a little shop that sold hot beverages and snacks. She glanced up at them long enough to see they weren't heading her way, and then returned her attention to whatever she was reading under the counter.

"They're in this building, but further up," Daisy said. "The elevators are over here."

The halls leading off the platform were clean but utilitarian, designed to handle crowds of people and clean up easily after they were gone.

When they stepped off the elevator several dozen levels up, they were in quite a different space. It was clearly a private space, narrower and more warmly lit. Some of the doors they walked past had little decorations on them, something about the occupants, their family, or their culture. Most had more of the silver snowflakes, some cut out and some printed on blue banners.

A few had little tables sitting outside the door with bowls of flowers or candles or candies. The sounds of one family dinner or another could just be heard through the doors, laughter and the excited chatter of children.

Scout's attention was caught by a particularly elaborate handwoven family crest hanging from one door when she nearly collided with Daisy's back. Daisy had come to an abrupt halt and was standing stock-still in the middle of the hall.

Scout looked over her shoulder and saw that the last door on the right was standing open. Not all the way open, but not quite closed, either.

The locking mechanism looked twisted, as if someone had forced the door open and it would no longer close properly.

"Daisy?" Scout whispered, clutching the leashes tightly to keep the dogs close. They were both sniffing the air; their ears twitched back in what she recognized as nervousness.

"Stay here," Daisy whispered back to her, then advanced to push the door fully open.

The apartment beyond was dark, lit only by the lights from the city streaming in through the windows. Daisy flipped a switch, but the lights still wouldn't come on.

"It's a trap," Scout said.

"More like a lure," Daisy said. "We were meant to find this."

"And do what?" Scout asked. She put both leashes in one hand, then found her light with the other and clicked it on.

"Go after Shi Jian," Daisy said. She had gone all the way into the room but looked back when Scout started shining her light around.

The room had been destroyed. Every piece of furniture was smashed, fabric torn to shreds. The computer unit built into the wall by the kitchen had been completely dismantled, components strewed everywhere. Even the bathroom looked like it had been methodically dismantled.

"Were they looking for something?" Scout wondered.

"Doubtful," Daisy said. "The Torreses don't have anything the Tajaki trade dynasty doesn't already know about. They just want it to look like some other crime happened, I guess. It wouldn't take much to make local security decide there was nothing worth investigating further. It wouldn't be odd to find anyone gone. People from other planets never stay here long."

"But how did they do this without anyone else in this building hearing?" Scout asked. She hadn't met any of them, and yet from the warm displays on their doors, they all seemed so friendly.

"They took their time," Daisy said. "It wasn't as violent as it looks. They probably took the Torreses away before they even started dismantling the place."

"Away to where?" Scout asked. "Do you think the McGillicuddys were here when they got here?"

"Back to her ship," Daisy said, "and I'm afraid so." She held up a scrap that took Scout a long moment to recognize.

Emma's scarf.

"Her ship," Scout started to say.

"We have to get up to the port," Daisy said. "Stars, everything is making sense now, and I really don't like it."

"What makes sense?" Scout asked, but Daisy was already pushing past her, running back to the elevators. Scout took another look around the apartment, saw an enormous box of energy bars left sitting in a ransacked cupboard, and grabbed it before running after Daisy.

"You need it," she said when Daisy glared at her from where she was holding the elevator door. "You can eat on the transport."

"It won't do more than take the edge off," Daisy all but growled, then took a deep breath. "Sorry. Clearly, I need to take the edge off. I'm getting cranky. Thank you, Scout."

"We take care of each other, right?" Scout said.

Daisy's face started to crumple like she was about to break down into tears, and Scout felt a rush of panic. But Daisy pulled herself back together, squaring her shoulders back and blinking hard.

"Yes," Daisy said.

They had to wait for two trains to come and go before their train arrived, but in that time, Daisy had scarfed down the entire contents of the box. Scout was nauseous just watching her, but also a bit in awe. How did she even fit all that inside her stomach?

But when the last bite was swallowed and the wrappers disposed of, Daisy was looking better. She still had dark circles under her eyes and a hollow look to her cheeks, but the gray color was gone from her skin, and her eyes had lost the dull sheen that had made her look like she was ready to give up on everything.

It was a short ride to the city center, then up an elevator back to the processing center. Daisy took Scout's arm, pulling her into a door she was certain they weren't meant to be using, then through a maze of narrow corridors and up stairs so steep they were nearly ladders.

At the end of it all, they were back in the very topmost room of the building, the one with the domed ceiling, the star-shaped one with all the ramps radiating out like rays from a star, leading to where airships docked.

"Which way?" Scout asked as Daisy looked up at a display board over one of the doorways out into the thick clouds that concealed all but the first few steps outside the building. "Did you come down in a harbor ship?"

"No, shuttle," Daisy said, her eyes darting over the long lists of ship names and arrival and departure times.

Then her eyes stopped on a name, and her shoulders fell. It was like her entire posture just collapsed in on itself.

"What is it?" Scout asked. "They're gone?"

"Not just the shuttle," Daisy said. "The ship itself."

"Gone?" She bit back the words "without me?"

"Leaving," Daisy clarified. "I'm sorry, Scout. I'm so sorry. I don't think Shi Jian was ever after you at all."

"What do you mean?" Scout asked. "They blew up the station and attacked me at the cabin. They chased both of us all over the mountain."

"All over the mountain," Daisy agreed. "Kept us busy. I don't think they found anyone in that apartment, as much as she wants us to think so. I think your friends were cleverer than that. They hid from her and her spies for days, but they've got them now."

"Why? If not to get to me, then why?" Scout asked.

"The Torreses are a far bigger problem to the Tajaki trade dynasty than you could ever be," Daisy said. "They've been hiding for years. Evading capture. Outside of the courtroom, they're like ghosts. I think Shi Jian was looking for the McGillicuddys to use them as leverage against the Torreses. I don't think she expected to get them both. I don't know."

"I led her to them," Scout said, starting to put the pieces together herself.

"She knew I was watching," Daisy said. "She knew what I would assume, that I would want to get to you. She manipulated me, and I fell for it. All of that psychological testing… she reads me like a book. I always discount that, but she does. I think it's such a victory that she can't just tell me what to do and I do it, but if she can make me do what she wants by other means, I haven't gained a thing by fighting her. Nothing I can do will ever be unexpected to her."

"Look, this doesn't change anything," Scout said. "We still have to rescue my friends. That means getting to Shi Jian."

"It's impossible," Daisy said. "The shuttle is gone, and the ship is already leaving the harbor area."

"How fast?" Scout asked.

"What?" Daisy asked, blinking as if the question caught her off guard. "Not very. There are rules. The harbor is full of ships; the traffic is heavily regulated."

"Do you mean controlled? Like by someone here?" Scout asked.

"Yes, but what good does that do us?" Daisy asked.

"We might have a chance to slow them down and to catch up with them before they gun their engines," Scout said.

"How?" Daisy asked.

"Check those boards again," Scout said. "Where is the airship Hikosen?"

Daisy squinted up at the boards, then pointed to one of the ramps.

They both ran towards it, charging out of the doors and back into the cold, oxygen-starved atmosphere high over Schneeheim.

24

ALL THE TIREDNESS that had been dragging at Scout since they had left the Torreses' apartment was blasted out of her by the first touch of the freezing air outside. The cloud was all around them, coating her in a wet layer that hardened into ice almost instantly.

They still had their coats with them. They just didn't have any time to spare getting them out of the pack and putting them on.

They ran towards the end of the ramp, the massive outline of a balloon slowly emerging from the blowing wisps of white cloud ahead. They weren't too late.

Then Shadow barked his happy greeting bark. Gert, who saved her bark for enemies, nevertheless was hopping up and down in excitement. Then Scout saw her too: Minato, walking towards them down the ramp.

But Scout quickly realized that something was wrong. Minato was barely pulling herself along with her crutches, dragging her feet over the ground rather than stepping. Her head was bent down, but she looked up when she heard the dogs, and her expression was one of such weary sadness Scout felt her own heart squeezing tight in empathy.

"What is it, Minato?" Scout asked, handing the dogs' leashes over to

Daisy so she could keep them from jumping all over Minato as Scout moved closer, putting a hand on Minato's arm.

"My father," Minato said, and her body seemed to slump even further. "He's downstairs, in intensive care."

"Oh, Minato. I'm so sorry," Scout said. "Is he going to be all right?"

"They can't say. It will be hours yet before they even know if he's responding to the latest treatment. But I can't be with him. I'm not even still supposed to be here; I've exceeded my gravity time for the week already. But I can't just leave."

"That sounds really hard," Scout said. She could see that even the light pull of gravity on the ramp was exhausting Minato, and Scout suspected she wasn't even willing to sit down to rest. She looked like she had been pacing the ramp, waiting for news.

There was no kind way to tell her she was going to kill herself if she kept it up.

"Scout?" Daisy said. When Scout glanced at her, she tipped her head back towards the station, suggesting they find another option. Scout bit her lip.

They needed to get to Shi Jian, but just abandoning Minato felt like the wrong thing to do.

"What are you doing up here, anyway?" Minato asked, not having missed the exchange of looks between the two of them.

"Well," Scout said, not sure what to say.

"We need a ride," Daisy said. "Someone very dangerous is going to hurt a lot of people if we don't stop her in time."

"We can find another way…" Scout started to say.

"No," Minato said, raising her chin. "This is exactly what I need. Get on my ship. I'll take you anywhere you need to go."

"Do you need help?" Daisy offered.

"No," Minato said, turning herself around on the heel of one braced foot and marching with impressive speed to the end of the ramp, up into the gondola of her ship. Scout and Daisy got the dogs aboard, then closed the door behind them.

By the time they reached the bridge, Minato was already buckling herself into a support structure that now stood where her father's tank had been. This was more like a padded rail she could lean against, with a narrower padded semicircle that braced her up under her arms. She had tossed her canes aside and was just reaching for a lever. The docking mechanism, Scout realized, and she caught hold of the edge of a panel as the ship dropped out beneath her. The falling sensation ended in a stomach-roiling swoop as the balloon started to ascend, pulling the gondola up after it.

"Which ship?" Minato asked, bringing up a series of displays.

"The Ming Yue," Daisy said, moving forward to examine the displays. "There."

"I see it," Minato said, hands on the controls.

"It's nearly out of restricted harbor space," Daisy said.

"What does that mean?" Scout asked.

"It means they will no longer have to observe Schneeheim velocity restrictions. They will start accelerating. We'll lose them."

"They aren't there yet," Minato said. "Hold on. This is going to be bumpy."

Scout clutched the edge of the panel again, but when the floor first pressed up underneath her, then dropped away so suddenly she felt like she was falling, she opted to sit down on the floor instead, hugging both of her dogs close.

Daisy, on the other hand, had a manic grin on her face, leaning forward to watch the last of the clouds peel away from the viewscreen as Minato increased their acceleration.

Just as they started slowing down again, having reached the limit of what the balloon could do, she fired the rockets. Scout yelped even louder than the dogs as they were suddenly tumbling backward, the nose of the ship now the 'up.'

They piled on top of each other at the back of the cabin, narrowly missing a longer tumble down the hallway. Shadow was trembling, and even Gert seemed shaken.

Daisy was laughing. So was Minato.

Clearly, they were insane.

"How much further?" Scout asked when the acceleration finally stopped and they were moving at a constant velocity. She released the dogs, and they slowly settled to the floor close to the back wall. Not quite freefall yet.

"Nearly there," Daisy said, but then pointed. "You're going to run out of fuel."

"Yes," Minato agreed. "I have enough left to navigate to that ship's airlock, but this is as fast as we're going to get there."

Daisy studied the dot that represented the Ming Yue, then the dot that was their ship. "It'll be enough," she said with certainty.

"What about after?" Scout asked. "How are you getting back down?"

"Balloon," Minato said. "That, and gravity pulling me down. It will take a while, but I'll get there."

"But your father," Scout said.

"I can't help him," Minato said, her hands tightening on the controls. "But I can help you. And I need to be doing something helpful."

"Thank you," Scout said.

"Yes, thanks," Daisy added. "You have no idea what this is even all about, but you didn't hesitate to do your part."

"I don't know the specifics, but I know she arrived on a tribunal enforcer ship," Minato said, tipping her head towards Scout. "Whatever you're mixed up in, if it involves the likes of them, it's huge. And I don't get the sense you're on the side of the bad guys. The tribunal enforcers treated you with respect."

"Look," Daisy said, pointing to another screen. Minato looked at it, then moved it to the central screen and enlarged it. Scout didn't know what they were looking at. It was all scrolling data to her. But Minato's face hardened.

"What is it?" Scout asked.

"Their engines are warming up," Minato said.

"They'll be firing them soon," Daisy said. "How fast can you dock once we're alongside?"

"I'm the fastest," Minato said. No one who was bragging would do it with such a grim look on their face. Scout believed her absolutely.

Minato dismissed the data screen, and they were once more seeing the view from the nose of the ship. The Ming Yue was clearly visible ahead of them, the soft blue glow of its engines intensifying.

Scout looked away from that light. Even just looking at the color of it was making her head feel swimmy. She remembered her close encounter with a warp field back on the Months' ship. And that one had just been idling.

"Hold on," Minato said, and Scout looked up again as the ship around her lurched to one side. They were past the engines, matching velocity with the ship now. Minato reached for a different control and pulled a trigger.

Scout caught a hold of a panel just in time to keep from spilling to the floor again. Whatever Minato had done, it felt like they were a fish on the end of a line now, being dragged after the Ming Yue at high speed.

"Hold on," Minato said. At first, Scout thought she was giving that warning a touch too late, but then the airship starting bucking under her feet, up and down and side to side. The dogs yelped in protest.

"What's happening?" Scout asked.

"I've harpooned on to their ship," Minato told her through gritted teeth. "I'm reeling us in. Once we're locked down, I can extend the walkway and force their airlock open."

"Force it? How?" Scout asked.

Minato just gave her a maniacal grin. "Trust me. I've done this before."

Scout had a million questions, plus the image of Minato dressed like the pirates that flocked to the Months' court.

They had picked the right girl to ask for help, that was for sure.

Scout saw the side of the Ming Yue drawing ever closer on the viewscreen. Then the shaking ride was over as suddenly as it began, ending with a loud clang that echoed throughout the airship.

"We're docked," Minato said, turning to them with a proud grin.

"You're awesome," Daisy said. "We better hurry through the airlock."

"Yes," Scout said, running to collect the dogs.

The image of Minato's delicate airship getting bashed to pieces as the much larger deep space vessel accelerated to its full velocity wouldn't leave her mind.

They had to get off her ship so she could detach before that happened.

And even still, she was going to be left without fuel far from the harbor, in a much higher orbit than her ship was designed for.

"I'll be fine," Minato said, as if reading Scout's thoughts. "You two take care of yourselves. And the dogs, of course. I have a feeling you're the ones who are about to be in real danger."

"I hope we meet again," Daisy said, then sailed through the airlock, landing neatly on her feet the moment she reached the Ming Yue's artificial gravity.

"I hope your dad is okay," Scout said, pushing first Gert and then Shadow through the airlock to Daisy's waiting arms. "Be safe."

"You too," Minato said, giving Scout a little push out the airlock. Scout's feet pressed against the hull of Minato's ship and she launched herself down the white tube to the far ship.

The gravity grabbed her the moment she passed through the Ming Yue's hatch, and she somersaulted out of the way so that Daisy could slam the door shut behind her.

Scout scrambled to her feet and found a viewscreen near the airlock door. As Daisy spun the wheel to seal the door, Scout watched the airship fall away behind them.

It looked so small in all that black. She hoped Minato would be okay.

"Come on," Daisy said. "However Minato did it, it seems no one knows we came in through the airlock, but we can't stay invisible to the ship's systems forever. Let's get moving."

Scout unclipped the leashes from the dogs in case they need to run. Daisy dropped her pack to the floor and drew her gun. Scout did likewise.

Whatever they were about to face, cold weather gear and mountain climbing equipment were not going to be any help.

Scout was afraid the gun wasn't going to either. She had that feeling again, like she was about to find another layer above her when she was already in over her head. But there was nothing to do but press on.

Somewhere, the Torreses and the McGillicuddys needed her. She couldn't let them down.

25

THE HALL outside the airlock was dark, the only source of light a thin red line running along the walls at about the level of the handrails. Scout turned on her night vision, but it didn't help much—she could already see the general outlines—so she toggled it back off again.

Daisy took the lead, gun in both hands, although she kept it pointed down towards the floor. Scout mimicked her posture, assuming there was a reason behind everything Daisy did.

The dogs didn't like the dark. They stayed close to Scout's heels, sniffing the air but not making any noise.

Daisy paused when the hallway ended in a larger cross corridor. She looked both ways, but they both led off into a red-tinged darkness with no signs of doors or anything.

"Why is it empty and dark?" Scout asked in a whisper.

"Skeleton crew, probably," Daisy whispered back. "We never got off the shuttle, and we weren't told why. If this ship is uncrewed, that might be part of it."

"Doesn't she trust her assassins?" Scout asked.

Daisy's mouth twisted as she thought that one over. "I don't think that's it. There might have been someone else on the ship who she didn't want to know about her assassins. I don't really know."

"So which way?" Scout asked. Daisy looked both ways again, then picked the corridor on the left.

Scout was pretty sure it was a random choice, but she had no better ideas, so she just followed along.

This corridor ended in another, even larger one. The walls had two narrow bands of red lights running down them. But even with twice the light source, the hallway felt no brighter.

"Does it mean something?" Scout asked, running a hand over the two lines. Daisy just shrugged and took the corridor on the right.

The two-lined corridor ran on for hundreds of meters. They passed closed doors and other cross corridors with only the single band of light to guide the way, but Daisy didn't give any of them more than a passing glance.

Scout had a prickling feeling at the back of her neck, like she was being watched. She had had that feeling before, when she had been surrounded by assassins and hadn't known it. She kept looking back, focusing intently, when suddenly her glasses seemed to understand she was looking for possible surveillance. They flagged several dots at regular intervals down the corridor, then labeled them as cameras tracking their motion.

But there was no sign of life.

"Someone somewhere is watching us," Scout whispered.

"Most assuredly," Daisy agreed.

A sudden rush of dizziness nearly sent Scout stumbling over her own feet. She stopped and pressed one hand over her eyes; the other braced against the wall. She felt like she needed that wall's help in staying upright.

"What is it?" Daisy asked.

"I feel weird," Scout said.

"Weird how?" Daisy asked, looking around as if for something in the air itself.

"Weird like..." The words floated away from her. Daisy was still speaking, but those words floated away, too. Like Scout was hurtling through space too fast for speech to catch up with her.

"Scout!"

Scout snapped back into the moment to find Daisy violently shaking her by the shoulders.

"Sorry," Scout said.

"What happened?"

"I think we're moving," Scout said. "Hyperspace. I have a weird reaction to warp fields."

Daisy gave her a skeptical look but said nothing.

"I felt it on the Months' ship when I was looking at their engine, and they weren't even moving at the time. Then again on the tribunal enforcers' ship when we were in hyperspace. But that was just like being a little off, and I didn't even know why until it was over. Nothing like this."

"Stronger engine," Daisy said, although she still looked like she wasn't sure she believed what Scout was telling her. "Different effect."

"Maybe."

"Are you okay now?" Daisy asked.

Scout blinked, and for the brief moment when her eyes were closed, she felt that rushing, falling, plummeting-forward feeling. But she still had her hand on the wall. The wall gave her strength.

She swallowed hard and nodded.

Daisy kept looking at her as if waiting for Scout's head to explode or something.

"Tell me if anything changes," Daisy said. "I need to know when I can rely on you and when I can't."

"I'm good," Scout promised. "I'm getting used to it. I've got it under control."

Daisy nodded, then continued down the hall. Scout took a breath and followed, working hard to ignore the feeling that she was moving so much faster than one step at a time.

The corridor ended in a short flight of steps up to a pair of double doors that stood open as if someone was expecting them.

Daisy held up a hand, and Scout took that to mean she wanted to go on ahead and look around before Scout and the dogs followed. Scout nodded, then squatted down and grabbed the dogs by their collars to hold them still.

Daisy still had her gun pointed to the floor, but her arms were more rigid now, like she was prepared to lift and fire inside of a breath if she had to. She stepped back against the wall, then slid slowly over to the doorway to peek inside.

Scout watched Daisy's face as she looked around the room. She saw her eyes widen momentarily and her body twitched as if she were catching herself before rushing in. Only after a thorough sweep of the entire vicinity did she take a step further inside. Then more looking, then another step.

Then she waved for Scout and the dogs to follow before moving quickly out of sight.

Scout let the dogs go and drew her own gun again, just in case. The dogs ran up the steps to find Daisy.

It took Scout a little longer. Looking down at the steps made that forward-tumbling, rushing feeling come back again, and she was certain she was putting her feet down wrong, that she was about to fall trying to go up three very shallow steps.

She closed her eyes and ran up them. When she reached the doorway, she opened her eyes and saw Daisy kneeling on the floor beside a body. She was touching their neck even as her gaze was still sweeping the room around her, looking for threats.

Then Scout took another step inside the room and saw there was more than one body on the floor. Far more.

Daisy rolled the body she was touching over onto its back, and the hair that had been covering the face fell away.

It was Mary Grace Torres.

"No!" Scout cried.

"She's not dead," Daisy said. "None of them are. Just unconscious."

Scout was standing over Daisy now and saw that the other bodies were John Carlo and Emma and her sons.

"Why are they tied up if they're unconscious?" Scout asked.

Daisy stood up and shrugged. She was about to say something when the doors hissed shut.

It was such a soft sound, and yet it reverberated around them.

"Dogs!" Scout called, panicked that they might have been in the hallway. Shadow ran to her side. Then, a moment later, Gert appeared from behind a workstation.

Licking her lips. Did Scout even want to know what she had gotten into?

"Were they gassed?" Scout asked, as another wave of panic hit her. Were she and Daisy about to join the others unconscious on the floor?

"I don't know," Daisy said, looking up at the vents in the ceiling over them. Then she walked over to one of the workstations. "This is a navigation station. That one there is communications. And this is flight control. We're on the bridge."

"But there's no viewscreen," Scout said. It looked like any other room to her, if dark and lit only by the red lines that still ran along all the walls.

"It's not necessary," Daisy said. "But someone must be here running things."

"A crew?" Scout said. She saw no sign of anyone hiding behind any of the workstations or crouching under the panels.

"I think a single person could do it," Daisy said. "They'd have to be able to hold a lot of tasks in their head at the same time and prioritize them appropriately, but it could be just one."

"You are correct," a woman's voice rang out, and the lights blazed to life. Scout threw an arm over her eyes. She hoped Daisy's eyes adjusted faster than hers.

"Shi Jian," Daisy said.

"I almost thought you two wouldn't make it," Shi Jian said. Scout lowered her arm, still blinking furiously as her eyes adapted to the bright light. Shi Jian was just a black outline in a white space for the first few blinks. Then the room gained detail and Scout could see Shi Jian's face.

She was smiling at them, like all of this was some delicious game.

Then she realized what Shi Jian had just said.

"You wanted us here?" she asked.

"Both of you, yes," Shi Jian said. She was leaning one hip against the corner of a workstation, arms folded, no sign of a weapon anywhere.

But anything could be tucked away under the loose folds of her cloak.

"So you really were after me the whole time?" Scout asked.

"So simplistic, your thinking," Shi Jian said, still smiling. "This isn't the sort of game where I can only make one move at a time. And as Daisy said, I can give many tasks my full attention at the same time and prioritize them accordingly. I promise you, everyone who is on this ship is here for a specific reason."

"The kids?" Scout asked, pointing at Emma's sons.

Shi Jian just shrugged, her smile never faltering.

Scout had a sick feeling that they were going to be recruits.

"Who do you work for?" Daisy demanded.

"Please," Shi Jian said. "That's not what we're here to discuss."

"What are we here to discuss?" Daisy asked.

"Why, a team-up," Shi Jian said.

"What?" Scout asked, not even sure she had heard Shi Jian correctly; the idea was so outrageous.

"I've refused your orders once," Daisy reminded her.

"I know," Shi Jian said. "I can't order either of you about. You never took to the training, and Scout is far too old to start the conditioning now."

"So what are you saying?" Daisy demanded.

"That you two should join forces with me. Willingly. Whole-heartedly."

"Why would we do that?" Scout asked.

"Because if you don't, I will destroy you," Shi Jian said glibly, and the smile cranked up another notch.

"Why would you even need us?" Daisy asked.

Shi Jian shrugged. "Obviously I don't, but I like you both. I don't really want to destroy you. I'd rather keep you as sort of an advanced class. A more freethinking class than the younger cadre, but that could be a good thing. The more indoctrinated have limitations."

"There's no way we're ever agreeing to that," Scout said, then glanced at Daisy. "Right?"

"Right," Daisy said and raised her weapon.

Shi Jian put up a hand. "You're not going to shoot me."

Daisy fired a shot. Shi Jian, who had seemed to be so casually leaning against the workstation, was suddenly backflipping over the panel to land on her feet on the other side. Daisy's shot hit the screen on what she had said was the communications station, sending sparks everywhere.

Shi Jian laughed. "Nice try."

"Try, try again," Daisy said and fired another shot.

Shi Jian danced out of the way, and the bolt struck the wall where she had been.

Scout raised her own gun. When Daisy took her next shot, Scout would try to head off Shi Jian's dodge.

Not that she thought she'd have more luck, not with her lack of actual shooting skill, but they might get lucky.

"You can't hit me," Shi Jian said. "It would be better not to try. We are on the bridge, you know."

"The systems have backups," Daisy said.

"Of course they do, but not all in the same room," Shi Jian said. "So tell me, how fast can you run?"

"If you're going to destroy us, then just do it already," Daisy growled.

Scout really wished she hadn't said that.

But Shi Jian looked positively delighted. She made a sweeping gesture with her arms, directing their attention to one of the work-stations.

As if that gesture had been some sort of command, the screen in the station flickered to life. Scout and Daisy glanced at each other. Then, as Shi Jian took several steps back, they stepped up closer to see what was appearing on the screen.

Whatever camera the screen was broadcasting from was moving through a dark room, large but cluttered with great mounds of junk under tarps coated with dust. The camera tipped down, and a hand appeared, dragging its fingers through the dust on one of the mounds, then another.

The screen was showing them something through someone else's eyes, and Scout was afraid she knew who.

The motion stopped, and the person pivoted to look back the way they had come, occasionally looking down at a gun they were spinning over and over around one finger, a lazy gesture with a very deadly object.

Scout took a step back and then another. She looked around until she found Shadow and Gert both tucked together under one of the other workstations, sniffing at the fried wire smell that permeated the bridge from the still-smoldering communications station and looking up at Scout with big, trusting eyes.

Gert's ears perked up, and she tipped her head as if trying to suss out what Scout was thinking.

Scout turned back to Shi Jian, who was watching her with a mad gleam in her eyes. She knew exactly what Scout was about to say, but she was going to make Scout say the words, anyway.

"Stop it," Scout said. "Please."

Shi Jian pulled a face meant to be read as sad and shook her head.

"Daisy, please don't look," Scout said, putting a hand on Daisy's arm. "Please. I can explain, but not like this. Please, trust me?"

Daisy looked over at Scout, those all-too-familiar eyes very carefully blank. Whatever she was thinking, she wasn't going to let Scout see a bit of it.

Then she looked back at the screen. Just in time for Scout's grand entrance, slingshot in hand and already firing towards the person whose eyes had recorded everything.

Clementine.

26

DAISY'S cold eyes stared fixedly at the screen showing her the last moments of her sister's life. Scout wasn't even sure if she knew what she was seeing. Her expression never changed, but she never looked away.

What was she thinking? Why didn't she look at Scout even once?

Scout backed away, step by step, until she stood between the nook her dogs were hiding in and the rest of the room.

Gert looked up as she heard herself growling fiercely on the playback. Scout flinched at Clementine's shriek of rage and pain, then turned her face away as the version of her from the past begged Clementine not to shoot her dog.

"Please, Clementine. It's just a dog."

Scout looked to Daisy one last time. If there were any lingering doubt, Scout saying her sister's name would surely have killed it.

Then the Scout from the past rushed at the screen, and there was a confusing moment, a scuffle that ended in a cry of pain.

Then the screen went black.

"Daisy," Scout said softly. She saw Daisy's shoulders flinch, but she didn't turn, just kept staring at the now-blank screen. "I'm sorry."

"Sorry?" Shi Jian repeated. "Why be sorry? It was her or you. We all know that."

"She was going to shoot Gert," Scout said.

"And after she shot Gert, she was going to kill you far more slowly," Shi Jian said. "Granted, that didn't appear in my little video, but I think we all know it's true."

Scout wished Shi Jian would just stop talking.

She wished Daisy would start.

"I wanted to tell you—" Scout began.

"No, you didn't," Shi Jian interrupted. "You absolutely did not. You wanted to go the rest of your lives never speaking a word of it."

Scout felt her cheeks burning. Because when Shi Jian said it, Scout was afraid it was actually true.

"See, I know you both so well," Shi Jian went on. "I know what you're thinking. I know what you're feeling. Like Daisy here. My star pupil. She knows it was supposed to be her down on that planet infiltrating the governor's mansion. Not Clementine."

Scout looked at Daisy, who had shifted from staring at the screen to staring at the floor, but her right hand was clutching her pistol so tightly it was starting to tremble.

If Shi Jian kept talking, would she shoot at her again?

Scout still had her own weapon in her hand. Maybe this wasn't over yet.

"Nothing in Clementine's short, tragic life was supposed to happen to her. But it did. I don't think any of the three of us believes in something as banal as fate, do we?"

Daisy's eyes darted up to Shi Jian, but only for a fraction of a second.

"A million, million causes having a million, million effects. No one can untangle those threads, and even if some are thicker than others, there's never really one core reason for anything. Daisy knows this."

Daisy didn't respond. Shi Jian slipped out from around the workstation, gliding across the room to stand before Daisy with the graceful nonchalance of a cat.

"Your parents are taken from you, your sister is separated from you in that terrible orphanage, all because of a war that should never have happened in the first place. Employees of a corporation declaring war on a different department? Insanity!"

Daisy made another darting glance up to Shi Jian, who was once more leaning a hip on a workstation and looking down at Daisy with her arms crossed.

"There is no one person who can take the blame for that sequence of events. And if you can't blame anyone in particular, blame everyone. That's always been my motto. We're all in this closed system together; we all share the causes and effects. Everyone is to blame. Am I right?"

This time, when Daisy looked up at her, she didn't look back down. Her blue-gray eyes stayed on Shi Jian's with a mute intensity.

"Blame everyone," Shi Jian said again. "But maybe start with her." She raised a hand to stab a finger at Scout. "She's the one who took a blade and wedged it in the one place—the one place!—she knew your sister would never recover from. The one place she was sure would kill her. She did it deliberately. Her intent was very, very clear."

Daisy said nothing, but the muscle in her jaw tightened.

Shi Jian seemed to be waiting for something, but Daisy still didn't move. In the end, she stopped pointing at Scout and gave a little shrug before refolding her arms.

"Maybe the dog then," Shi Jian said. "The big black monstrosity that tore the flesh from Clementine's arm. Her augmented flesh, the one that gave her heightened reflexes. Enhanced strength.

"A greatly intensified sense of touch."

Daisy winced.

"Yes, you know what I mean," Shi Jian purred. "We feel everything, you and I. Everyone else just thinks we're invulnerable, able to recover from almost any injury. They don't know about the pain. We feel it so much more than they do. I'm sure you remember waking up from all the surgeries in unending agony. You might have thought it was just because you were a kid, why it felt like the worst pain imaginable. Maybe you thought, well, it's just because I've never been hurt like this before."

"But I was an adult when I got my augments. I can heal from nearly any wound, and I have. Over and over again. It never stops hurting. All of our jacked-up nerve endings turn on us when we're in pain.

"Your sister's last moments were nothing but agony. I daresay, even as furiously, fabulously stubborn as your sister was, in the end, she welcomed death. Just to end the pain that *she* caused her."

Shi Jian was jabbing her finger again. Daisy's eyes followed the path it was indicating, then moved back to Shi Jian.

"The girl, or the dog?" she asked.

Shi Jian hesitated, and something almost like confusion made her smile waver for just a moment. Clearly, this wasn't a question she had been expecting.

But she decided how to respond quickly enough. "Both. If you can't blame one, blame all, remember? Come on," she said, pushing away from the workstation and slapping her hands together. "Help me throw them out an airlock."

Daisy's eyes narrowed suspiciously.

"I know it won't mean we're friends," Shi Jian said. "It's just a job that needs to be done, so why not do it together? You need your revenge, and I need rid of this meddlesome girl. And I've never liked dogs."

Daisy's tight grip on her pistol loosened. Then she lifted her hand, spinning the gun around her finger several times before tucking it back in her holster.

Shi Jian grinned even more widely than before. "You taught Clementine that," she guessed.

Daisy just shrugged. "Is there a closer airlock than the one we busted into?"

"Of course," Shi Jian said. "That little pirate, thinking she was so clever busting you in through what's basically the trash chute. I did notice that, by the way. But no matter. There's an airlock just through there, by the escape pods for the bridge crew. And don't ask if we can just jettison them out in a pod to slowly die alone in the void. As lovely as that sounds, under the current circumstances, I really want to be sure she's gone. Shall we?"

Daisy turned and walked to Scout, deliberately not looking at her.

"Daisy, no," Scout said, moving between the girl and her dogs. "Don't do this."

Daisy didn't answer, just put one hand on Scout's shoulder and shoved her aside.

Scout went flying across the bridge, landing in a heap on the floor. And she doubted Daisy had used even a fraction of her augmented strength.

And Daisy was as weak as a newborn calf compared to Shi Jian. Scout was grossly outmatched.

Daisy stooped and held out her hand to Gert, who smelled it, then licked it. Her tail thumped happily on the floor. Daisy scratched at her ear, then reached for her collar.

"Run, dogs!" Scout screamed as she scrambled to get back to her feet. That feeling of movement that didn't sync with what was actually happening was making it hard to get up. "Run!"

Shadow tried to dart around Daisy, but Shi Jian was right behind her and scooped him up.

Gert's tail stopped wagging. Shadow yelped as he tried to twist out of Shi Jian's arms and Gert growled a low warning growl.

Daisy lunged forward and snatched a hold of Gert's collar, hauling her out to where she could pick her up.

"No!" Scout cried, running after them. She tried to pull on Daisy's arm, but it was immovable. Gert whined pitifully.

Shadow yelped in pain, and Scout ran at Shi Jian. She didn't even think about it, just jumped on the woman's back and pressed the barrel of her gun to Shi Jian's temple.

She pulled the trigger, but not before Shi Jian directed a single elbow back sharply, sending Scout back down to the floor, wheezing in pain. Shadow remained pinned tightly in Shi Jian's other arm.

Scout couldn't draw a breath, and her vision was flooding around the edges with an alarming dark red color. The world was spinning and tipping back and forth, even looping over on itself, and she could taste bile at the back of her throat.

She was vaguely aware of Daisy's feet moving past her, of the door hissing open and then closed again.

Scout pushed herself back onto her feet and stumbled after, keeping her eyes closed until she stopped moving. That helped her walk without falling, but when she opened them to see where she was, the world was still twisting around. She caught glimpses of things and tried to assemble them into a picture inside her head. A small, narrow hallway dotted with round hatches. The escape pods, Scout assumed.

At the far end of the hallway, an airlock. Scout took a deep breath, then looked again. The inner door was already standing open. Shi Jian tossed Shadow inside, and he managed to land on his feet but retreated to what he thought was the safety of the far wall, barking and snarling and generally warning Shi Jian to stay back.

Not knowing Shi Jian was no longer the real danger.

"Please, Daisy! Don't!" Scout cried.

"She said something similar to your sister there at the end, didn't she?" Shi Jian said, looking back at Scout as she still fought to draw a breath in. Her diaphragm was spasming arhythmically. She took two more stumbling steps, but stopped when her vision started spinning again. "Better watch your back," Shi Jian said to Daisy. "She must have a knife somewhere in all those pockets."

Daisy turned to look back at Scout. Gert in her arms was squirming with all her might, but Daisy's arms were immovable.

"Gert," Scout said miserably. She couldn't help her dog, and Gert couldn't help her either. Not this time.

Daisy hugged Gert a bit tighter, burying her nose in the fur at the back of Gert's neck just like Scout loved to do.

"Let her go," Scout said, her voice shaking as much with rage as pain and exhaustion.

"Let her go?" Daisy repeated.

"Let. Her. Go."

Daisy shrugged. "Okay."

Scout couldn't quite understand what was happening. Daisy pivoted away from Scout, taking a step closer to Shi Jian, who was practically cackling in delight.

But those cackles died away as forty pounds of angry hound from hell landed on her, driving her back into the airlock.

Then Daisy stepped back, the end of Shi Jian's cloak slipping away from something Daisy held in her hand.

A grappler. She had taken it from Shi Jian's belt.

"Scout, call the dogs!" Daisy commanded.

She didn't have to tell Scout twice.

27

SCOUT TOOK A DEEP BREATH, ignoring the stabbing pain like a knife between her ribs at the point where Shi Jian's elbow had struck her, and yelled as fiercely as she could.

"Shadow! Gert! Come!"

Shadow darted past Shi Jian's flailing arm to get to her, ears flat against the sides of his head. He was deeply upset.

Gert stayed where she was, standing on Shi Jian's chest, her growl building to an intensity that had every hair on Scout's body standing on end.

Shi Jian swung an arm and sent Gert flying back down the hall. Scout rushed forward to catch her before she hit the ground. She managed to break the big dog's fall, although she didn't think she had so much prevented any injuries as spread them out between the two of them.

Shi Jian leaped to her feet with a snarl but was blasted back into the airlock when Daisy fired the grappler.

That was never going to hold her. Already her talons were tearing at the thick webbing.

But Daisy didn't expect it to hold her for longer than a second. That was all she needed to slam her hand down on the button to close the inner door.

She turned to Scout, eyes bright with triumph. But before she could say a word, just as the door was slamming shut, an arm snaked out, and those talons wrapped around Daisy's throat.

"Daisy!" Scout screamed, running to Daisy's side. Behind Daisy, she saw the door close down on Shi Jian's arm. The edge dug in, tearing the black fabric of her sleeve, slicing into her flesh.

Then it stopped. And started to open again.

"Obstruction detected," a voice from nowhere told them.

"No!" Scout yelled, trying to catch the door with her hands and force it to close again.

It was useless. The voice kept repeating over and over, "Obstruction detected," but the door never stopped. Scout pounded at it with her fists in frustration.

"Scout," Daisy croaked as Shi Jian's fingers tightened around her throat. It took a moment for Scout to realize Daisy wasn't looking at her, but at the panel behind her. She spun around and slammed her hand down on the close button, but the door continued to open.

"Man. You. Al." Daisy's eyes were starting to bulge, her face turning a very disturbing deep red, but still she fought to get the syllables out.

Then Scout realized what she was trying to tell her. The panel had another smaller button labeled "manual override."

Scout slapped her hand down on that. The door shuddered, then started to close again. Scout started to turn to help Daisy, but the moment she stopped touching the button, the door started opening again.

Daisy managed a truncated rasping breath, but she wouldn't be able to hold out much longer. Scout put both hands on the button and leaned her whole weight into it. She wasn't sure if that would help. It didn't seem to make it close any faster. But neither was it stopping.

Inside the airlock, Shi Jian was still tearing away at the webbing with the talons on the hand that wasn't around Daisy's throat. She would be free sooner than the door would be closed.

"Daisy?" Scout called.

Daisy made a little *urp* of sound. She had both hands around Shi Jian's wrist but didn't have the strength to break her grip.

The closing door drew closer, and Daisy turned to face Shi Jian, bracing one foot on the wall and the other on the closing door, then leaned back with all her strength. Scout cried out in alarm. Was she trying to help Shi Jian strangle her faster?

Then the last of the webbing gave way with a rip, and Shi Jian shrieked in triumph.

Or started to. Her triumphant shriek twisted off at the end to one of confused surprise.

And Scout finally realized what Daisy had been doing. She hadn't just been bracing her feet to pull back on Shi Jian's arm; she had been using her feet to pull the door closed just a little bit faster.

The opening wasn't large enough for Shi Jian to get through, even when she turned her body sideways.

Then she tried to let Daisy go, to retract her arm, but Daisy held on tight, pulling back with all her might so that Shi Jian's shoulder remained in the door's path.

Shi Jian realized what was happening and screamed in rage. Scout leaned harder on the button, and the repeating voice explaining about the obstruction it was detecting seemed to her ears to acquire a shrillness, as if the disembodied voice were growing alarmed.

Then the door was biting into Shi Jian's flesh again, higher this time. And the door didn't stop.

It took an eternity, but the motor was relentless. Finally, the last bit of metallic bone was severed, and the door shut with a final *thoom*, cutting off Shi Jian's cries.

Daisy fell to the ground, inadvertently hugging the severed arm.

Scout sagged against the control panel, more exhausted than she had ever been in her life.

The world was still lurching around her. She wanted to be sick.

"Scout!" Daisy said, throwing the arm aside. "The other door!"

There was an echoing boom, then another. Shi Jian was going to batter her way back inside the ship.

Scout forced herself back to her knees, found the control to open the outer door, and jabbed at it.

The blows against the door abruptly stopped. A moment later, there was another more distant *thoom*.

Then nothing. Just blessed silence.

Scout slumped down to sit with her back to the wall, but Daisy was already on her feet, scrambling to run back to the bridge.

Shi Jian wouldn't die just because she was exposed to the vacuum of space. Scout knew that for a fact. And if she had gotten hold of the outside of the ship, she would crawl around until she found another way inside.

Scout forced herself up and ran after Daisy.

"Is she out there?" Scout asked.

Daisy was studying first one monitor and then the next. At last, she jabbed a finger at one. "There she is!"

"Where?" Scout asked, looking over Daisy's shoulder.

"See her? She's tumbling through the void."

Scout leaned closer and could just discern a dot of movement. Shi Jian, dressed all in black, was hard to pick out from all the black around her, but occasionally her tumbling form would blot out a star behind her.

"Serves her right," Scout said. "She hurt my dog."

"I'm sorry, Scout," Daisy said, her voice thick with unshed tears. "I didn't see another way."

Scout reached down and gave Daisy's hand a squeeze.

Then they both gasped as the star field on the monitor was suddenly blotted out by something much larger than Shi Jian's body.

"What is that?" Scout gasped. "Not a tribunal enforcer ship."

"No, definitely not," Daisy said. "You can still see stars through a tribunal enforcer ship. They let all light pass through. This looks like it's sucking up all the light around it. What the hell is it?"

Shi Jian's body was impossible to make out against that background. Where had she gone?

Then, as quickly as it appeared, the mysterious thing was gone, and the stars were back. And none of them were being eclipsed by a tumbling body anymore.

Scout felt another rush of world spinning and tried to sit down until it passed.

She missed the chair, landing on her tailbone with a jolt. Dogs were all over her, licking her anxiously. She tried to pet them, to give them a little reassurance, but the fragments of her vision blurred together and she couldn't tell just where they were.

"Scout?" Daisy called from a great distance.

Scout couldn't summon words. She couldn't even think them.

She kind of thought she slumped to the floor, but it was hard to tell. The world was just dogs, anxious for her attention.

Suddenly a foul smell filled the world, expanding inside her sinuses; there was no escaping it. Scout sat up and scrambled back, trying to get hands up between her and that smell.

"It's okay, Scout!" Daisy said. "It's not a stim. Just a whiff of ammonia. How are you doing?"

Scout put her hands down and looked around.

The world had stopped dancing that psychedelic dance.

"What happened?" she asked.

"I dropped us out of hyperspace," Daisy said. "Shut down the warp field. But you still weren't coming out of it, and we're nearly back to Schneeheim, so I thought, why not try the medical bay?"

"Oh," Scout said, then realized the dogs were still near her, looking for her attention. She gathered them both close. "Thanks."

"I'm so sorry," Daisy said.

"I'm sorry too," Scout said. "We have a lot to talk about."

"But we have business to take care of first," Daisy said. "Shi Jian."

"We still don't know who she is or who she works for," Scout said. "But I'm very sure she's not dead."

"No, she's not," Daisy said. "This isn't over yet. I tracked that mystery ship's trajectory. It's possible they might stop somewhere and change course to throw us off, but I don't think so. I'm pretty sure she's headed to Galactic Central at full speed."

"Isn't that the logical place for her to go?" Scout asked.

"There's more," Daisy said and helped Scout up to sit in the chair.

The screen in front of her was some sort of schematic of a building, with lines pointing to different places.

Connecting those places with pictures of Geeta, Seeta, and Emilie.

"What is this?" Scout asked.

"It's what Shi Jian was working on when we boarded," Daisy told her. "She's setting up an op. To get inside the compound belonging to the Tajaki sisters known as the Months. To take out your friends."

"I'm sure their security system is state-of-the-art," Scout said.

"I'm sure it is," Daisy agreed. "We both know it won't matter."

"Can we send a warning?"

"Sure," Daisy said. "I doubt it will help."

"Then what?" Scout asked.

"We need to get there ourselves. In this ship, nothing else is faster. And we need to leave now. Shi Jian already has an hour head start on us. Even that might be too much."

Scout rubbed the back of her hand against her mouth. The ammonia smell was still lingering in her sinuses, and the back of her throat had a bitter burn to it from the bile. In fact, her entire body felt battered and bruised, and she was so very tired.

But she had to save her friends.

28

DAISY CARRIED the McGillicuddys and the Torreses one by one into an escape pod, buckling them into the seats that lined the space.

"You're sure they'll be okay?" Scout asked. Daisy gently rolled John Carlo's head back into the restraint and velcroed it into place.

"They'll be fine," she said. "The doctors in processing at Schneeheim are more than qualified to wake them from whatever drug Shi Jian gave them." She stepped back from John Carlo's seat, then looked them all over one last time before stepping out of the escape pod. She saw the worry still on Scout's face. "This is for the best. Shi Jian left all her little spies behind on this world. It's better for your friends if they don't know where we went."

"I wouldn't put it past any of Shi Jian's recruits to torture someone endlessly for information they never even had," Scout said.

Daisy gave a curt nod. "You're right. This is better for us. The one thing we have going for us in stopping Shi Jian is that she doesn't know we're planning to. We have to run swiftly and silently. Your friends will be taken care of. The McGillicuddys will get a marshal guard after this kidnapping attempt, so they'll be safe, and the Torreses will surely have some similar form of government protection only in Galactic Central in their case."

"The court case is starting up," Scout guessed.

"Barring any more last-minute delays," Daisy said. "All the Tajaki lawyers excel at stalling, but they're running out of objections. The legal proceedings are going to begin. That's no longer stoppable. Which is why I'm so sure Shi Jian is going to start taking out witnesses. We have to get there. We have to hurry."

Scout sighed but nodded, and Daisy fired the escape pod. They watched it fall away behind them on the little monitor until it was no longer visible.

Then they went back to the bridge.

"You're sure you can do this on your own?" Scout asked.

"Drug you? I've had training," Daisy said, looking over the medical equipment she had hauled in from the medical bay. The bed had been reconfigured into more of a reclining chair mode, and a blanket lay folded across the foot.

The number of monitors arrayed around it was surely excessive. How many things could actually be going on at one time in her body that anyone would really need to know about in such detail?

"I meant fly the ship," Scout said. "We destroyed some things in the fight, you know."

"Nothing crucial for our trip through hyperspace," Daisy said. "I'll be fine. Are you ready?"

Scout looked at the reclining chair and hugged herself tight. She was, as always, in space, feeling a bit cold. But that wasn't the chief reason she was wrapping her arms around herself so closely.

They would be in hyperspace for days. And the little research Daisy had done into what was happening to Scout hadn't turned up much, only that it was rare and little studied.

Not so rare that no one else had experienced it. Scout took a little comfort in that.

But definitely so rare that no one with her sensitivities had gone tearing across the galaxy in a ship with this new kind of super-fast warp engine.

"I'll be watching you constantly, Scout," Daisy said. "If you look at all uncomfortable, I'll take us out of hyperspace. We'll come up with another plan."

"There is no other plan," Scout said. "We agreed. We don't know who else we can trust. We sent a warning to the Months, but without a response from them, we don't know what they're doing. Bo is still in hyperspace, and we don't know who he can trust. It's just us. We have to get there. And this is the fastest way."

"I wish there were another way," Daisy said.

"Yeah, well," Scout said. But still didn't step any closer to that chair. "I'm really sorry about your sister."

Daisy's eyes widened, as if she was shocked that Scout would bring it up, but then she looked down at her own hands holding the injector she was waiting to administer to Scout.

"I didn't know how to tell you I already knew," Daisy said. "I wanted to, but I just didn't have the words."

"I should have told you first," Scout said. "I should have found another way to protect myself from your sister than killing her."

"What you killed wasn't my sister," Daisy said, still looking at her hands. "And what Shi Jian first molded and shaped into a killer... I don't think even that was my sister anymore. She lost herself, that first night in the orphanage. And nothing I did after that night ever helped her find herself again."

"She might have. One day," Scout said.

"Maybe," Daisy said. "I don't know. It's not worth dwelling on, I don't think. It's in the past, unchangeable. We have to focus on what's ahead of us, what we can change."

"The other kids that Shi Jian has indoctrinated," Scout said. "Maybe we can still save them."

"Maybe," Daisy said. "But first, we save your friends."

"Then win our day in court," Scout said.

"And then save our planet," Daisy finished. "Wow. We have quite the to-do list."

"Time to check off the first line item," Scout said and climbed onto the reclining chair. Shadow immediately hopped up out of nowhere to sit beside her, tucking himself close to her side. Gert, who only needed to be near her, not smothering her, flopped down near Scout's feet.

"You'll be awake," Daisy said. "Aware, but like from a distance. You won't be able to talk, but I'll be able to tell if you're in distress. We're just trying to calm the hyperactive part of your brain that is trying to track your motion when we're in hyperspace, and hyperspace doesn't like to be tracked."

Scout tried to muster a smile. None of Daisy's explanations for why Scout felt weird made much sense to her, but Daisy understood it. That was all that mattered.

"Hit me," Scout said, baring her biceps for the injector. "And wake me on the other side."

Heavily sedated and strapped to a bed: not how she had imagined her arrival to Galactic Central.

But at last, she was heading there.

CHECK OUT BOOK SIX!

The Travels of Scout Shannon concludes with Book Six, At Galactic Central.

Galactic Central, a collection of floating cities in a vast, manmade, planetless cloud. Scout Shannon longed to see it since she first heard of it. This place long represented her shining future.

But in her less shiny present, she reaches it by smuggling herself aboard a cargo ship and hides in the lower sewer-like levels of the most opulent of the floating cities. Teams of girl assassins still hunt her. Worse, her friends are in danger and don't even know.

Scout has to save her friends, because saving her friends means saving her entire planet from enslavement to the Tajaki trade dynasty. Caught between two sides of that dynasty, with a mysterious third party desperate to remove her from the galaxy, Scout is in way over her head. But with her friends, she just might see a path to victory for all of them.

"At Galactic Central" the sixth and final book in "The Travels of Scout Shannon" series, a young adult science fiction novel for fans of plucky heroines, girl assassins, political intrigue, and loyal dog sidekicks.

At Galactic Central, the final book in the Travels of Scout Shannon. Check it out!

NEW SERIES: THE FORGOTTEN PLANET

Coming soon from Ratatoskr Press Books, the new YA sci-fi series THE FORGOTTEN PLANET starts with book 1: Raiding the Forgotten Derelict.

History sleeps beneath them all, but only she sees it.

Lafayette Eloi always knew her parents thought differently from others. They kept their books buried beneath her mother's house. They spoke an old language in the dead of night, whispering behind closed doors and bolted shutters. She grew up in a village where no one was related to her, and she never knew why.

Then, after her mother died, her father came to fetch her. Now she and her mother's dog assist her father in his work. The work discussed in whispers in the dark. The work that had cost Lafayette so much all her young life.

But now she learns just how much her father's work means to their entire world. Only no one knows anything about it. Only her father. And only Lafayette.

Because the work that consumed her father's entire life and her mother's too now nibbles at the fringe's of Lafayette's own life. And she cannot refuse its call.

Raiding the Forgotten Derelict, first book in the new YA sci-fu series THE FORGOTTEN PLANET, available in September 2024 from Ratatoskr Press Books.

COMPLETE SERIES: THE RITCHIE AND FITZ SCI-FI MURDER MYSTERIES

The Ritchie and Fitz Sci-Fi Murder Mysteries starts with Murder on the Intergalactic Railway.

For Murdina Ritchie, acceptance at the Oymyakon Foreign Service Academy means one last chance at her dream of becoming a diplomat for the Union of Free Worlds. For Shackleton Fitz IV, it represents his last chance not to fail out of military service entirely.

Strange that fate should throw them together now, among the last group of students admitted after the start of the semester. They had once shared the strongest of friendships. But that all ended a long time ago.

But when an insufferable but politically important woman turns up murdered, the two agree to put their differences aside and work together to solve the case.

Because the murderer might strike again. But more importantly, solving a murder would just have to impress the dour colonel who clearly thinks neither of them belong at his academy.

Murder on the Intergalactic Railway, the first book in the Ritchie and Fitz Sci-Fi Murder Mysteries.

COMPLETE SERIES: THE TRAVELS OF SCOUT SHANNON

The complete six-book series THE TRAVELS OF SCOUT SHANNON begin with book one, Under Falling Skies.

Scout Shannon's whole family died the day the Space Farers dropped an asteroid on their domed city. Now she lives alone, out in the wild with only her dogs for company. She prefers it that way.

But Scout finds herself at a crossroads. One road leads back to a quiet life snug under the protective dome of a city. The other road leads to a life in the rebellion, a life of adventure and excitement but also danger. Dare she try to find the rebels hiding in the hills?

Then a chance encounter with a stranger from the other side of the galaxy threatens to derail what remains of Scout's life. The entire galaxy awaits her, if she survives the next four days.

"Under Falling Skies", a young adult science fiction novel, set on a remote planet with a distinctly Old West feel. For fans of gunslinging women and young girl assassins. And dogs.

Under Falling Skies, the first book in THE TRAVELS OF SCOUT SHANNON, available everywhere now.

SCI-FI SERIAL PODCAST!

Check out my new monthly podcast of serialized science fiction: THE TALES OF THE CHAI MAKHANI TRIO!

Elyot loathes the massive Commonwealth ships that hover menacingly over his home world of Adghal. He hates the Commonwealth enforcers who harass the populace even more. But with his mother missing and presumed dead, Elyot keeps his head down and strives to avoid notice. And he succeeds until the day two strangers enter his life...

New episodes of this sci-fi serial drop every 1st of the month.

Now streaming on Apple Podcasts, Google Podcasts, Spotify, Stitcher and more. Also available in eBook and print everywhere books or sold. For a complete episode listing, check out the page on my website.

ALSO FROM KATE MACLEOD

Love heists and capers? Then check out my new series, THE VIC HARPER CAPERS. The action starts with the novella THE THIRD POLE JOB.

Vic Harper and her gang retired wealthy from their life of thievery and heists. Whether in a luxury condo overlooking the river in Minneapolis or in a modernist mansion built into the side of a mountain in Colorado, life comes easy now.

Perhaps too easy.

When an old friend asks for a favor his niece, Vic and her mentor Chase Woodward leap at the chance to relieve a little of the boredom. But a quick bit of B&E in a wealthy suburb of Chicago leads to an even greater challenge.

The prize? Nothing much. Just the opportunity to level a playing field for their friend's niece.

But the heist? May prove to be their toughest ever. Because to get to the prize, they'll have to climb a mountain.

And not just any mountain. Their prize waits on the summit of Mount Everest.

THE THIRD POLE JOB, the first novella in the Vic Harper Caper series. For those who love capers, heists and other impossible missions.

ALSO FROM RATATOSKR PRESS

Also from Ratatoskr Press, The Witches Three Cozy Mystery Series by Cate Martin, a mix of mystery and magic that begins with Book 1: Charm School.

Amanda Clarke thinks of herself as perfectly ordinary in every way. Just a small-town girl who serves breakfast all day in a little diner nestled next to the highway, nothing but dairy farms for miles around. She fits in there.

But then an old woman she never met dies, and Amanda was named in her will. Now Amanda packs a bag and heads to the big city, to Miss Zenobia Weekes' Charm School for Exceptional Young Ladies. And it's not in just any neighborhood. No, she finds herself on Summit Avenue in St. Paul, a street lined with gorgeous old houses, the former homes of lumber barons, railroad millionaires, even the writer F. Scott Fitzgerald. Why, Amanda can practically hear the jazz music still playing across the decades.

Scratch that. The music really, literally, still plays in the backyard of the charm school. Because the house stretches across time itself. Without a witch to protect this tear in the fabric of the world, anything can spill over. Like music.

Or like murder.

The complete series is out now, and it all starts with Charm School.

FREE EBOOK!

Like exclusive, free content?

To get two prequel short stories to THE RITCHIE AND FITZ SCI-FI MURDER MYSTERIES as well as a bonus prequel novelette to the completed six-book series THE TRAVELS OF SCOUT SHANNON, signup for my monthly newsletter at KateMacLeodWrites.com.

Thank you!

ABOUT THE AUTHOR

Photograph © 2016 Jonathan Conklin

Kate MacLeod has written stories which have appeared in Analog, Strange Horizons and Mythic Delirium, among other places. She is also the author of two young adult science fictions series: The Travels of Scout Shannon, and The Ritchie and Fitz Sci-Fi Murder Mysteries. She also contributes to a serialized science fiction podcast called The Tales of the Chai Makhani Trio. She currently lives in Minneapolis, Minnesota.

Find out more about the author and sign up for her newsletter at KateMacLeodWrites.com.

ALSO BY KATE MACLEOD

Novels

The Slums of the Solar System:

Mitwa

The Mars of Malcontents

The Whole World for Each

Books 1-3 Box Set

The Travels of Scout Shannon:

Under Falling Skies

In Quaking Hills

Among Treacherous Stars

Against Impassable Barriers

Over Freezing Altitudes

At Galactic Central

The Travels of Scout Shannon Books 1-3

The Travels of Scout Shannon Books 4-6

The Travels of Scout Shannon Books 1-6

The Ritchie and Fitz Sci-Fi Murder Mysteries:

Murder on the Intergalactic Railway

Murder in the Skies

Body in the Catacombs

Death on the Summit

An Undiplomatic Murder

A Lethal Betrayal

The Forgotten Planet

Raiding the Forgotten Derelict (Forthcoming September 2024)

Sci-Fi Novellas

The Intergenerational Tree

I Rise into a Daybreak

Caper Novellas

The Third Pole Job

The Twelve Days of Christmas Job

10-Story Collections

Tales of Blood and Ink

Tales of Old Gods and New

5-Story Collections

Tales from Heian-Kyo and Others

Tales from the Edges and Ends

Tales from Forgotten Days

Tales from Ancient and Future Times

<u>Tales from Across Space</u>